Ramonst

A.F. Knott

Hekate Publishing

2 Lydiard Green

Lydiard Millicent

Wiltshire SN5 3LP United Kingdom

admin@hekatepublishing.com

https://www.hekatepublishing.com

Dedicated to Annie Margaret Francis.
Thanks to Rowan Leigh and Hekate Publishing.
Thanks to Catherine Adams for the initial enthusiasm.

1

RAMONST

The ear started to hurt as soon as the propeller job took off. My mother handed me a stick of Juicy Fruit and said,

"Yawn as hard as you can."

That didn't work so I put my head down on the tray table, drew up the shade and looked at the window panes. Dad explained that an airplane window had two panes; if there were only one and that one was to crack, the person sitting next to it would disappear like a piece of Kleenex held up to an Electrolux hose. Oxygen masks would drop, Dad said, with everybody jerking sideways but not being sucked out as long as they were wearing seatbelts.

I pulled the shade down and listened to my mother. She was speaking about Uncle Andy. When he was my age, he had a dog that foamed at the mouth.

"Everywhere that dog went, Andy would follow him."

"Why did he follow him?"

"I don't know why. Every single day after school he followed him, repeating his name. I heard him saying it: Ramonst, Ramonst, Ramonst, Ramonst, Ramonst. For months this went on."

Ramonst did not sound like a dog's name to me, so I asked

if she was sure about that.

"Yes, Ramonst. That's the name he gave him. Repeated it over and over and over and over and over. One day Andy came home from school and started in on the dog, but Ramonst didn't move. He sat in the hallway staring at Andy then started foaming at the mouth. Mother had Ramonst shot, and they sent his brain over to the University of Tennessee. After running all the tests they still didn't know what caused Ramonst's foaming."

I couldn't stop thinking about Ramonst after my mother told me that. Even though she said they never found out what caused the foaming, I asked:

"What do you think caused Ramonst's foaming at the mouth?"

My mother spoke quickly.

"I think Ramonst couldn't take all that is what I think. Dear Lord, every day I'd hear him saying it: Ramonst, Ramonst, Ramonst, Ramonst, Ramonst. I would foam too.".

2

REMEMBERING THAT FAR BACK, PEACH ICE CREAM, AND MAY TARWATER

I still couldn't hear out of the one ear, but knew what to expect: My ear had to creak like an old door, the creaking would feel like a splinter being yanked then everything would return to normal.

My ear creaked as soon as the propeller job touched down in Knoxville and Nana was standing by the gate, puffing out her cheek, waiting for a smacker. The first time I saw Nana, the sidewalk at the Knoxville airport had been hot as an oven. Sunlight flooded the road, the parking lot, and everywhere around her.

Every few months my mother reminded me: *I hadn't said one word to Nana for ten whole years before that day. When I was a little girl, she used to tie me up in the closet and wouldn't let me out. You became our ambassador.*

Each time Nana picked us up at the airport she liked to tell the story of the first time she and I met:

I opened my arms, and you just ran into them.

Whenever Nana began that story, my mother said,

Of course, you can't remember that far back.

3

I remembered everything that far back. I remembered Nana's green Olds the very first time I saw it, as big as a New York City Checker cab. My mother became angry each time I told her that I could remember.

No, you can't remember that far back. Nobody can. You were too young.

But I could: Nana had been kneeling with her arms out, and my mother whispered:

That's your grandmother. Go run up to her and give her a big hug.

Nana had puffed air into her cheek and called out,

Oh Honey, come and give Nana a nice big smacker!

I remembered even farther back than Nana's first smacker but didn't tell my mother. Instead, I wrote it down. I made a list of memories as well as things that people said, especially the things people said over and over. Dad gave me two yellow pads from his desk; one for book reports, one for writing down memories and what people said. My mother found the what people said pad and kept it, so Dad gave me another and told me:

Hide it in a place Mum won't find it.

~

We stopped at the homemade peach ice cream stand before pulling out onto the Oak Ridge highway. Once back in the Olds, with all three of us holding our cones,

Nana turned in her seat, puffed air into her cheeks, and said:

"Oh honey, your cousin Brodie's bringing you his medical school skull! Since you're a full eleven, Brodie said you're old enough to look at one."

Last summer, I had been a full ten, old enough to drive my mother's Comet all the way to Ivy Point and back. This year, I turned full eleven, old enough to look at Brodie's medical school skull.

"Your Uncle Andy and Aunt Adair, Shaw and the twins are all up at the house as well as your Uncle Gavin and cousin Duncan. Dixie drove clear across the mountains last night with Lillian and Cameron."

"And they all just can't wait to see you!" My mother crunched her cone. She had told me not to say a word to anybody about Aunt Adair going over to Hawaii and picking up Uncle Andy from the hospital.

Uncle Andy's men had been sneaking their tents at night, trying to kill each other with hand grenades. He's as afraid of his own men as he is the Viet Cong.

Uncle Andy had been in both Korea and Vietnam and just about had it after his jeep ran over a land mine.

Uncle Andy had to pretend that he was dead, you see, and I think that did something to him, after everything he had been through.

My mother took a bite out of her cone and turned to Nana.

"I think you should tell Rodney what you told me about Munro's boy."

Nana's cone crunch was so loud and sudden that I jumped. After that, she spoke with peach ice cream dangling off her chin.

"Yes honey, it's best to steer clear of Munro's son Clyne. They say he may have shot a boy out of a tree over at Bonnet Lake, but we don't know if he did that."

"Oh, of course, we know, mother. Everybody knows. Clyne's been bragging about it. Dear God, it was just so sad about the little boy."

"Well, he's always just so polite with me."

My mother turned her head and stared at Nana.

"Mother. Andy told me that there was nothing the Sheriff could do. They had no proof, but everybody in town knows. I can't even bear to think about it. They said the boy had climbed into the tree to try and get away. They said he was just a little thing. His mother lost her husband the year before, and all she had was that little boy. No, there is something wrong with Clyne. There always has been. He cuts the heads off cats."

"Rindy Anne." Nana used her deep voice and nodded in my direction.

I already knew Clyne cut the heads off cats. Last summer Nana told Munro to pick up a mother cat who had just delivered her kittens under the azalea behind the back porch. That same day, I brought my F8F Bearcat out to the sandbox when Clyne stepped out of the woods, dropped a bag in front of the swing set and pulled out the orange cat.

I need for you to pin its goddamn legs down for me.

When I saw how Clyne was holding the orange cat, I couldn't move my feet, as if somebody had poured cement into the sandbox. Clyne dragged the cat over to the slide and held one of its legs down with his boot. After that, the cat wouldn't stop screaming. I felt my head spinning on the end of a rope. Clyne put his heel on the cat's head, then pulled out his pocket knife, opened it with his teeth and sliced the cat's belly open. The cat screamed and clawed Clyne's leg and was still screaming while Clyne sawed its head off.

I felt like vomiting for the rest of that morning and couldn't stop thinking about the sawing. I pretended nothing had happened and imagined again and again that same orange cat moving her kittens into the woods before Clyne ever showed up.

The day after the sawing, I had run out the front door and jumped off the porch before I spotted Clyne standing by Nana's holly bush. I wouldn't have come outside if I had known he was standing there. My feet went out from under me and my hands burned against the gravel when he took a step closer and whispered:

See no evil; speak no evil; hear no evil.

I knew what that meant because Dad had once demonstrated how the three Chinese monkeys put their hands over their ears, eyes and mouth. He had told me the story of the morning he walked over to his barbershop at the hotel on 7th Avenue. Men in black coats had come up beside him just before he went in. Dad and the men entered the lobby at the same time. One of the men turned to Dad and said:

The man who speaks too much will never have it easy. But whoever is deaf and blind and mute will live in peace for a hundred years.

After the man had told him that, Dad turned around and walked back to the apartment. Dad said he had been very lucky. On that same day, another man got shot having his haircut at the same barbershop. After finishing the story, Dad stood in front of the Zenith and showed me what the Chinese monkeys did.

My mother crunched her cone.

"Munro was hoping Andy could get Clyne into the Army, but Andy told Munro that he wouldn't do it. Andy said the Army wouldn't take Clyne. Clyne's off, you see. Uncle Andy told Munro the Marines might take him. Poor old Munro. He tries, you see."

I swirled my peach ice cream, curled it then bit off the tip of the curl. I had Clyne to worry about again. Before getting on the propeller job, I only had my summer book report on *The Arabian Nights* to worry about, and nothing else.

My mother was almost finished with her cone and said, "Don't talk to Clyne. If he comes up to you, walk away. Everybody knows what happened and dear God, now that other thing I was telling Dad about. There's no end to it. Clyne's off, way off. He's out of control. Andy said there is going to be trouble about that recent thing. Even Munro is afraid of Clyne. He told Perseus, 'I'm afraid of him.' I think Munro knows everything. He would have to know, wouldn't he? Poor old thing. It must be hard. Afraid of his very own son."

Nana said, "Well, like I said, Clyne is always just so polite with me.

~

Dad never went to Tennessee but enjoyed listening to my mother describe everything that went on down there. My mother told him about *the other thing* one night while the two of them had been sitting on the living room sofa and I had been holding a Matchbox car race on the kitchen table. I heard the whole story.

May Tarwater knocked on mother's back door and said she'd seen Clyne raping the middle Willoughby sister Kezia down by the tadpole pond. Dear God in heaven.

When Dad heard my mother say that, he said *Gee Gods*, put his tea cup down on the living room table and rubbed his chin.

May exaggerates just to stir things up, you see. Oh, but she knows EXACTLY what she's doing. Kezia is the one with the big chest and Clyne isn't the only one in town who's had her. Andy calls her the town pump.

Dear God, if it weren't for those teeth, she'd be a knockout. Adair had been sitting right at the kitchen table when May said that to mother and had me laughing, you know, the way she imitates May making her sounds. Gavin says she sounds like a quarterback hup hup HUP HUP. I nearly laughed myself to death the way she told it: 'Mrs. Matthews, that Presley boy raped Jemima Willoughby's sister down by your fountain.' Dear God in Heaven, doing it right by Tinker Bell's Fountain. It's all too much. I couldn't stop laughing.

Old May limped her way up Nana's driveway and sounded like a truck engine, *hup hup HUP HUP*. She twisted while she walked, the way a slug twists the second salt hits it. She twisted, talked, walked and limped all at the same time with her one bad eye pointing toward the dogwoods, the good one aiming straight ahead.

Old May wears eight coats, even on the hottest day of the summer.

Old May wore every coat she owned because someone had stolen her clothes one day while she was out delivering her newspapers. Old May told Munro that she knew who did it and was *fixing on killing that person.*

This happened over two years ago, but she'll remember it and wait for an opportunity. That's how they are up there. They remember.

Poor old thing.

Gavin thinks it was Munro's boy who stole her clothes. He's broken into miner's homes and taken their guns before. Munro always has had to cover for him, you see, leaving the things he's taken in plain sight on the side of the road so the miners wouldn't come for Clyne.

I'll bet May knows it's him that did it. She'll stand out there in the woods and watch. I've seen her out there. You think she's not paying attention, but oh yes, she is. Shrewder than you'd think but has the one eye that goes out sideways. Gavin told her he would take her to Nashville himself to get it fixed, but she didn't want to go. That's how they are. Suspicious. She would have such pretty features too if it

10

weren't for that eye. She's a product of incest, you see.

Every summer, my mother explained to the cousins that Old May was a product of incest.

She's a child of incest, you see, a product of her father. She has that eye that goes out like that.

Last summer the cousins had been sitting around the red checked kitchen table eating Nana's gingerbread when my mother said,

Old May is a product of her father.

Right after we finished our gingerbread, Duncan jumped off the front porch and yelled,

Old May's a product of her father!

I yelled, *Old May's a product of her father,* and we both couldn't stop laughing after that. We yelled it out again and again then really couldn't stop laughing.

Munro had heard us yelling it, came over and said we were both going to hell. Every year Munro told the cousins not to yell out certain things and that if we did, the devil was going to reach up out of the ground and drag us down to hell with him.

He's just trying to protect you. Religion is all he has, you see, and he believes in his Bible to the letter. He's not a bad man.

Munro had been angry with the cousins most of the last summer because there had been a day when we all shot peas at Old May, and afterward she had walked over to him wanting to find us. She told Munro she was going to stab us with her butcher knife and asked where we were.

11

He told her he didn't know, so Old May started yelling. She thought Munro knew and wasn't telling her. Munro had to climb back into his truck and drive away because Old May was following him around the garden swinging her knife.

That woman will slit your throat at the drop of a hat.

Every day Old May walked down from the mines, collected the Press and Tribune then followed Tennessee Avenue all the way over to the south side of town. She walked up Nana's drive, cut around the side of the house and put two papers behind the screen door before walking up to the Florist Shop to deliver Perseus a Tribune. Her last stop was always the Willoughby's house on the top of the hill. At the end of each day, she walked all the way through town and back up into the mines.

My mother told me Old May always kept a transistor radio with her.

Somewhere under one of her coats is a transistor. You used to be able to hear it playing while she was walking up the driveway. She would hum along.

I wanted more than anything in the world to hear Old May's transistor. Each summer, whenever she came up the path alongside the house, I ran upstairs, stood by Nana's open window, and held my breath but could never hear it. Old May was always making too much of a commotion when she limped past.

3

TUBE SWALLOWING, THE INCARNATION OF EVIL, AND THE LOOP

When we finally drove past Bonnet Lake, I craned my neck to examine every single tree I could, trying to figure out which one the boy had climbed before getting shot. Nana turned in her seat and puffed air into her cheeks.

"Oh, Rodney, I'll be fixin' to swallow that old tube right soon."

Nana swallowed her tube every eight weeks because of the strictures growing in her esophagus. Her tube was mercury lined and cut through the strictures like butter. She kept her tube in the downstairs bathroom chest, second drawer from the top. Every day last summer, I pulled open the drawer, and either studied the box itself or lifted the lid off to examine the tube. All the cousins knew where Nana's tube was kept and liked to look at it but not as much as I did.

Watching Nana swallow her tube was as nerve wracking as encountering what Dad called the incarnation of evil in my nightmares.

Every summer, on tube swallowing morning, my mother

and I woke up early and went downstairs to the kitchen. Nana always pulled a chair up next to hers beside the kitchen table and patted it. My mother would sit in the kitchen doorway no matter what Nana said.

I can't stand to watch, but I know we have to. It's just so dangerous letting her do it by herself.

"I had to swallow that old tube just before you came and I'll have to swallow it before you leave, Lord have mercy. Rodney, I am just so glad that you'll be with me. I'm not sure if I would be able to do it another time without you sitting right there at the kitchen table. It's just such a comfort to know you're there and watching."

I wasn't going to say a word to Nana about tube swallowing for the rest of the summer and hoped she would forget all about it until after we left.

~

Last winter I became fed up with the incarnation of evil showing up in my nightmares and decided to do the opposite of what it expected. Whenever I found myself in that same room with the furniture covered in white sheets, I stretched out my arms and dared the incarnation to do something. That worked. Evil ended up either becoming confused or trusting me.

The song *Jesus Loves Me This I Know* also worked against the incarnation. Mr. Barnes, our Bible School teacher, told us the story of John F. Kennedy's PT 109 sinking and how the Pacific Islanders who found him sang that song with the Marines on the rescue boat.

The only thing I liked about Bible school was singing and stamping our feet to *Yes, Jesus loves me, yesss, Jesus loves me, YESSS, Jesus loves me, for-the-Bible-tells-me-so!*

Duncan sang *Jesus Loves Me Yes I Know* so loud and angry that I wouldn't be able to stop laughing once he started. He bent both eyebrows inward until they almost touched and yelled at the top of his lungs:

FOR THE BIBLE TELLS ME SO!

My mother told me no one could change their dreams while they were still inside of them but I could, and I practiced doing it every single night. My mother refused to believe that anybody could or that it worked for me, so she stayed trapped in her nightmares. I tried to tell her how to do it, but she wouldn't listen.

~

Once we got off the highway, we took the right turn after the Crystal Drive-In and followed the Loop. Tennessee Avenue shot straight off Main Street, passed Nana's house after a mile then curved around the bend at the Willoughby's place to become the Loop. The Loop threaded through the back of town and came out by the Crystal. We used it as our shortcut to get cheeseburgers. On one side of the Old's window nothing but trees could be seen, only now and then a driveway. The driveways were nothing but wedges cut into the thick woods. The trees pushed ragweed as tall as I was, up to the side of the road where their stalks brushed against the Olds, *tick tick tick*, all the way around. Wrapping around every trunk were thick vines with their leaves of three.

Poison Ivy would strangle every single tree if it could, Nana said.

Gavin got up in there once, and his blisters were the size of grapefruits. We thought that was it; we had lost him. You can't even walk in those woods because of the poison ivy.

On the other side of the road, the ground dropped away with corn filling the little valleys, and tobacco growing in backyards and beside the barns. The smell of fire was always hanging in the air with old trucks parked along the side of little roads shooting off the Loop. I never once saw any of them being driven and never saw people walking, only lights coming in windows at night, like lightning bugs. If I spotted a dog, I'd follow it as long as I could because it was unusual to see anything move at all. Year after year, we passed the same stack of tires and same rusty brown truck laying in a bed of goldenrod, one headlamp missing its glass, the other hanging down like a joke shop clown's eye on a spring. With the Old's window rolled down, you heard the tires rolling rough against the road, pressing down and turning. You knew the second we had a flat from the *ker-thumping*.

Never stop to change a flat out on the Loop. Keep driving on your rim until you hit Prager's Store and change it there.

Everybody knew if you stopped to change a flat out farther out on the Loop, before Prager's, the rednecks might drive by and shoot at you.

We took the Loop every time we picked up milkshakes and cheeseburgers at the Crystal. I loved pulling into the Drive-In with all the cousins in the backseat more than any other thing I could imagine. The happiest I've ever been in my life was seeing the Crystal curbside waitress carrying our tray of food out to the car. I ordered a vanilla malt and cheeseburger every single time and my mother would roll her window halfway down so the waitress could hook our tray over. My mother would then take our cheeseburgers off the tray, and I'd watch those cheeseburgers as she passed them one by one to all the cousins. I'd watch her take the milkshakes off our tray and hand those out one by one as well. I'd unwrap my cheeseburger and start eating it bite by bite, examining my cheeseburger after each bite to gauge how much I had left while I'd pull vanilla shake up through the straw. At the Crystal, it was hard to pull the ice cream up. I had to pull hard and keep pulling then start tilting the cup and shovel it in. The straw and the cup gurgled at the end while I vacuumed up every last bit of shake. My mother would place our empty cups and empty wrappers on the tray, the waitress would come, take it all away, and we'd pull out.

As soon as we turned onto the Loop, my mother said,

"Mmm mm. Brings back memories. Do you remember the Loop, Rodney?"

Of course, I remembered the Loop and didn't need to answer.

"The Holy Rollers all live up in here, and the Klan lives a little farther out."

Nana spoke to my mother in a voice so low it sounded like

someone had put a water bucket over her head.

"Rindy Anne, nobody like that lives out here."

"Oh Mother, please, they're all rednecks up in there."

The way my mother said *they're all rednecks up in there* sounded like Munro needed to get out on the Loop and smoke the rednecks out like he smoked the yellow jackets out over Nana's back door. Every summer, yellow jackets crawled out of a little crack in the wood over the frame, flew away, flew back, landed and crawled inside the crack. The cousins never got to see Munro smoke the yellow jackets out because Nana lied to us over what time Munro would come to do it:

Sometime tomorrow afternoon.

Munro always smoked the yellow jackets out before the cousins woke up and Nana would only tell us he'd done it after we had finished our Cream of Wheat.

You can all come over to the back door and look through the screen.

Big piles of yellow jackets lay on the back porch with one or two flying back to the nest and hovering. The ones without a nest flew up to the crack, hovered, backed up, then flew away. Nana locked the back door because the yellow jackets were dying and still angry.

Munro told me: I use my Winstons to smoke them out. You had to have served in the military to know how to do that.

When he sat and smoked, Munro picked pieces of tobacco off the tip of his tongue as well as spat little pieces out between his teeth. Munro knew how to work his cigarettes. I always tried to imagine Munro smoking the yellow jackets out with his Winstons and could never figure out how he did it.

4

THE RABBIT, ROCKING PERSEUS, AND THE DEN

The Olds turned up Nana's driveway between the two stone pillars and started bouncing over the cobblestones. Dogwoods were lined up like soldiers holding swords over our heads, and I could see Nana's house sitting like the Queen of England on her throne, right through the middle of the trees.

It had been the biggest stone house in East Tennessee in its time. They don't build stone houses like that anymore. Daddy went into the mountains and picked all those stones out HIMSELF.

At the top of the drive, Munro's truck was sitting right behind Uncle Gavin's LTD, and my mother's Ford Comet was waiting for her under the Tulip tree beside the picnic table. Nana's front door still shined from shellac and the chairs on the front porch were still chalk white. Munro had put so many coats of white primer on the porch chairs that you could sit and roll paint between your fingers to make little animals. Right after my grandfather died, someone pulled up, loaded the front porch furniture onto their truck and drove away. Nana had iron ones made up at the mines that were too heavy to lift or even slide. Munro put the new coat of paint on every spring along with shellacking the doors and polyurethaning the floors.

Adair had been sitting on the steps when we drove up.

"Rodney honey, all your cousins are up at the Florist Shop just waiting to see you."

The first thing everybody saw coming through the front door of Nana's house was the back wall of the dining room with the three wooden paddles. Each of my uncles hung their paddle on the wall right after it had been split in two over their backside. Each uncle had written the date of their spanking in ball point pen under the crack in the wood, then signed their name.

This paddle was cracked over Gavin Matthews on July 26, 1944.

Each paddle was made of quarter inch plywood. Their spankings had been a lot worse than ours were now. My mother told me her brothers were each proud of their paddles, and that's why they hung in the dining room for all the cousins to see. One of my uncles, Brodie's father, had died. His paddle had been cracked five years before any of the others had.

That's because he was the meanest.

The cousins never ate at the dining room table and were not allowed to sit on the dining room chairs. We ate either at the kitchen table or, on special occasions, like the night after tube swallowing, in the little room past the refrigerator with its window facing the garden.

Through the living room door, the two brass pokers lay against the fireplace bricks and looked to have been polished. The broom, shovel, log grabber, and bellows hung on the stand where they had been since last summer. I loved playing with the bellows more than anything in the world, but Nana wouldn't let the cousins touch the fireplace utensils. When Nana was sleeping, my mother sometimes let me sneak in to play with the old radio.

She'll know it if you've touched anything else.

The twirling brass cactus ashtray sat on the living room table; beside that, the violet glass goblet. Wax bananas, oranges, and grapes rested in the violet glass bowl beside the violet glass goblet.

That's real Tennessee cut glass in there. You can't find that anymore.

The Nutcracker lay on its copper plate beside the silver cigarette case.

Walking down the hall, I brushed my fingers along the balusters, one after another. Munro had taught me all the parts of a staircase and let me watch when he put a volute on top of Nana's newel.

Munro could build you a house from a tree branch, but he's as lazy as they come.

I turned my head and had a look into the kitchen at the red checked tablecloth, Nana's stove, and the copper pots hanging on the overhead rack. Out the kitchen window, Nana's lilac and boxwoods stretched all the way back to the Florist Shop. The den door was straight ahead of me, beside that Uncle Andy's room then the downstairs bathroom where Nana kept her tube. All the doors glistened with shellac. There was one thing I had to check before I went upstairs. I tiptoed into the bathroom and lifted the commode lid: Empty. When Nana went to pick us up at the airport, someone must have flushed. The downstairs commode always contained one of Nana's snakes, whether it was day or night. We never knew why she didn't flush.

And it's getting worse the older she gets. Munro has to be called in once a week now to unstop the downstairs plumbing. He hates doing that. Hates it. I've heard him in there cursing, working the plunger. I would curse too.

Nana never admits that she leaves her snakes in the downstairs commode. One day when all the cousins had been sitting around the kitchen table, my mother caught her red handed. My mother pretended that she didn't know that Nana had been in the bathroom doing her business until after she came back out and started beating eggs in a bowl. My mother got up, strolled into the bathroom, opened the lid and there it was.

She STILL didn't admit it. I called her in and showed it to her. I don't know WHY she doesn't flush. I think she's getting back at us. She's always been a little like that.

The downstairs commode was the first place on the Daredevil's Club list to check during family reunions. I wanted to check it right off the bat. If there had been a snake sitting there, I would tell the cousins as soon as I saw them.

All last summer, Duncan screamed, *Oh my GOD, Roddoh,* at the top of his lungs whenever he found one of Nana's snakes sitting in the downstairs commode and every single time he did, I couldn't stop laughing.

When I came out of the bathroom, I heard Uncle Gavin's voice in the den but swung around the newel, ran up the stairs, and down the hallway into my room. My BB gun was standing in the corner. All year I imagined carrying my

BB gun in one hand down by my side like the GIs on Combat did or, rest it over my arm like Chuck Connors, the Rifleman. I had lined up my little green army men on top of the living room couch in New York and watched how each had pointed their gun, imagining that I was pointing my BB gun in the same way. The army men laying down were my favorites, but these were rare. Shaw called them snipers. You were lucky if you found three snipers in any one bag. The kneeling soldiers were my least favorite because they tipped over too easily. After twisting the base, they would be ok for a minute then became lopsided again. I set fire to the kneeling ones. The soldiers standing up, holding their rifles against their shoulders were better than the kneelers but not much better: They stayed standing a little longer after you twisted them.

The den door was cracked open when I came back down, and even though Aunt Adair, Uncle Andy, and Uncle Gavin were all in there, I swung around the newel and ran back outside. I held my BB gun in my right hand then switched it over to my left. I knew the cousins were all up at the Florist Shop and wanted to see them but aimed at the florist shop sign and shot three times, hitting it on the third try. After that, I felt more like carrying my gun than shooting it. I cocked the forearm just in case, walked out into the front yard like Chuck Connors and froze: A rabbit, with its head down, was nibbling grass, straight ahead of me.

"Let me barr that right quick."

Clyne had come up behind me without making a sound.

My mother had said walk away but I couldn't. Clyne was standing right there, so I handed him my BB gun. Clyne aimed at the rabbit and fired. The rabbit rolled over two times and made a noise like one of Nana's pans scraping against her stove top. Clyne walked up to the rabbit, primed my gun and pushed the end of the barrel against its eye. The rabbit jerked right before Clyne shot. When it flipped over, the rabbit's eye was dangling on its cheek. The rabbit moved around in circles and sounded like a tea kettle. I needed to sit down. Clyne turned my BB Gun upside down and pushed the butt against the rabbit's head, and I heard gravel crunching while the rabbit turned and kicked its legs out like a frog. Clyne came down two more times on its head, cocked it again and, pressed it into the rabbit. He fired, cocked it, pressed it against the rabbit's head and fired one more time then picked up the rabbit by its feet. The rabbit jerked from side to side, so Clyne smashed it against one of the oak trees. I felt something on my face, wiped and looked at my fingers. My stomach started to move, and I needed to lay down. Clyne handed me my BB gun and said,

"Your granny doesn't like seeing a single rabbit so I may need to fetch that."

Clyne walked away, holding the rabbit by its legs with its eye jumping back and forth with every step he took.

I used toilet paper in the upstairs bathroom to wipe the fur and blood off the stock of my BB gun then watched the tissue turn around in the bowl. I ran the barrel underneath the bathtub faucet then got down on my knees and held my face under the stream of water, brushing at the spot where something had landed. After that, I stood my BB gun in the corner of my room hoping that Clyne would forget all about it. I looked out the window at him tossing the rabbit into the back of Munro's truck. He climbed into the cab, and I could hear Munro yelling at him all the way through my upstairs window. Munro was still yelling at Clyne when he started the truck. The truck sounded like a man stuttering as it pulled away.

~

"Roddoh!" Duncan stood in the driveway right underneath my window. "We're fixing to rock ole Perseus up at the Florist Shop! Even Lillian's up there fixing to rock him!"

Duncan and Shaw, who were three years older, both called Cameron and Lillian, *the good cousins* because they never rocked Perseus. I rocked Perseus but wasn't sure if Duncan and Shaw also called me a good cousin or not.

Swinging around the newel, I still didn't have time to say hello to the adults but ran out the front door, jumped off the porch and slid in the gravel.

"Ole Roddoh! Let's go rock Perseus!"

We walked down the driveway, and I glanced over into the front yard at the spot where the rabbit had been nibbling. I turned my head away then turned back and saw the same tree against which Clyne had smashed it. I didn't say a word to Duncan, but when we turned up the Florist Shop Road, I had to look down into the garden to keep from getting dizzy. The sun cut through the dark green woods like the trees had all been switched and were bleeding light.

We spotted Shaw, Cameron, and Lillian up ahead standing

underneath the Florist Shop. As soon as we showed up, the cousins started rocking Perseus, aiming one piece of gravel at a time toward the open Florist Shop window. While we waited for Perseus to stick his head out and yell, I started laughing and couldn't stop. Every time a piece of gravel made it through the open window, we heard *TICK* and knew it had hit something. I was having more fun than I ever had in my life with all my cousins rocking Perseus.

Rocking Perseus was a Daredevil Club dare and considered a *medium*. Jumping off the top of Nana's stairs was another medium. Hanging off the second-floor lip then dropping down was the first dare you did after joining, called *initiation*. After completing initiation, a cousin could begin making up other dares. Shaw was President and decided which rank to give each dare and if it was a dare or not. The Matthews cousins were all members of the Daredevil's Club. The Bass boys were sometimes members when they visited their grandma and grandpa across the street. Shaw wasn't sure about them being elected permanent members because they might tell or chicken out.

Another medium dare was jumping over the bumblebees nest beside the sundial or pouring water down their hole then waiting for them to come swarming out. Slightly bigger than a medium was laying on top of the bank above Tennessee Avenue and shooting peas at cars then ducking down behind the beech ferns. After shooting our peas, we'd roll away and run as fast as we could back to Nana's house. Another bigger than a medium dare was climbing the dogwoods over the driveway and waiting for Old May to walk underneath. We'd drop red dogwood seeds on her or make noises.

Old May hated the cousins and yelled out she was going to

slit all our throats with her butcher knife if she caught us. Waiting for her at the end of the driveway was considered a *big dare* because you never knew if she was already hiding in the woods holding either her knife or a broken bottle, and might jump out. Old May hid in the woods, popped out from behind trees and chased us when we least expected her to.

Now and then I stood by myself at the end of the driveway without telling anybody. I listened for sticks cracking or gravel crunching and felt what it was like to be worried that Old May might jump out and try to stab me to death.

Perseus finally stuck his head out the Florist Shop window and shouted: "You goddamn little sons of bitches!"

Perseus was skinny as a rail. His hair was black and shiny and looked like the claw of a hammer. He kept a can of black shoe polish in his shirt pocket and combed his hair with it while he made wreaths. Every time we rocked Perseus, he came to the window, his black hair glistening and shouted the same thing down at us: *You goddamn little sons of bitches.*

"Oh my God, there he is!" Duncan screamed. "Look at Ole Perseus up there. Oh my God, Roddoh, there he is. Look at him. Let's rock Ole Perseus!"

"I'm going to throw a hand grenade!" Shaw picked up a fistful of gravel and threw it through the Florist shop window. Perseus jerked his head back inside when he saw the hand grenade sailing toward him.

Tat tat tat tat!

Perseus stuck his head back out of the window.

"You goddamn little sons of bitches. Spoiled little motherfuckers! I'm going to tell your grandmother all you little shits been rocking her Florist Shop!"

Perseus loved cursing at the cousins through the Florist Shop window more than anything in the world. Every summer we rocked Perseus every chance we got. When we visited him afterward, he showed us everything he'd been working on that day. He called the supplies he kept on his table *all my goddamn shit.*

Duncan loved imitating Perseus and was good at it but imitating Nana talking on the hall telephone was his specialty.

All my goddamn shit. Did you hear Perseus say that, Roddoh? All my goddamn shit.

I loved to say *all my goddamn shit* as well and laughed my head off every time I said it, even if I was by myself.

Perseus worked with big blocks of Styrofoam, green sticks and wires, spreading them all out on the Florist Shop table. He carefully examined the flowers in his refrigerator, picked out just the right ones, then cut them with his pruning scissors. He'd arrange these cut flowers around the green plastic vines as well as tying them with wires to the thin wooden sticks he'd jam down into the Styrofoam blocks. At the end of the day, Perseus lined up all his wreaths outside the shop ready for customers to pick up and bring over to the cemetery or to the funeral home.

Perseus sometimes handed me a piece of Styrofoam which I enjoyed pushing my fingers into as much as I did pushing my fingers into the clay you dug up behind the greenhouse. Now and then Perseus would hand me one of his green sticks. Shaw taught me how to whip a green stick through the air, making it into a *slasher*. The green sticks made a loud *CRACK* when you broke them in two.

Nana told me that Perseus lived up the hill behind the Florist Shop. I looked hard but could never see a road or even a path, just thick woods. How Perseus went home each day interested me a great deal because I never once saw him do it. I couldn't help but think Perseus lived someplace else, not up the hill behind the Florist Shop. There didn't seem to be anything but thick woods and no man could make his way up through all that.

Where does Perseus live again, Nana?

Nana always nodded in the same direction up the hill behind the Florist Shop.

Right up yonder.

~

As soon as we came running back into the house after rocking Perseus, my mother waved me over from the den door and said Uncle Andy, Aunt Adair, and Uncle Gavin were all inside waiting to see me. During reunions, the adults sat in the den and either told stories about the Matthews family or sat still and didn't say a word. When Uncle Andy saw us all walking through the den door, he said,

"And here come the communists!"

My mother clapped her hands together.

"Oh yes, A, tell them about the communists. They must know what you went through. Let it out."

After that, Uncle Andy only said, "well."

My mother started telling the story, and I wasn't sure from the expression on Uncle Andy's face whether he wanted her to or not.

"Right after Uncle Andy's jeep road over the land mine, communists came out of the jungle and stood on top of it smoking cigarettes. Little A had to lay underneath his driver's body and pretend that he was dead. Dear God. Tell it to them just like you told me, A. He used humor, you see, when he told it, and had me laughing near half to death. You said they were just standing up there, *chong chong chong*. It was the funniest thing I ever heard in my life the way you told it. The communists were all smoking up there, thinking you were dead."

Uncle Andy said, "Yes, well, you know, my driver was hanging over me, and I could see the hot dogs and beans in his stomach that we had eaten before leaving the base. He was still holding his pack of cigarettes."

When Uncle Andy spoke, he started out with *well, you know* as if everything he said after that would be normal to say, but it never was. Examining his face didn't help figure out whether or not he was joking. Uncle Andy went on to tell us that he heard the communists running over the top of the jeep and that he had to stay stock still.

"And if one of them didn't reach down and take the dad gum cigarettes out of my driver's hand. I'm not sure if they even knew I was there. I think they must not have."

"Andy said they stood on top of his jeep talking *ching chong chong chong*, just like that, all of them smoking the driver's cigarettes. Little Andy thought that was it, didn't you A? With them standing right up there on top *chong chong chong* and little A lying underneath his driver, mm MM. Dear God in heaven, Andy, LAW!"

When my mother stopped talking, Adair said, "Then they just ran off into the jungle, didn't they, honey?"

Uncle Andy didn't say anything.

My mother said: "Gavin, you had better tell Rodney what you were telling me about Munro's boy."

Uncle Gavin had been a football star and a paratrooper then hurt his back and became a doctor. Uncle Gavin always started out with a *you know* when he took a syringe out from his black bag: *You know, this is just going to feel like a little bee sting.*

"You know, Clyne is someone you need to keep as far away from as you can." Uncle Gavin winked at me and laughed. "Even Munro was telling me that he knows something is wrong with him."

Your Uncle Gavin and Uncle Andy laugh at nearly everything because both have seen it all.

My mother liked telling the story of Uncle Gavin and Uncle Andy going to the whore house in Knoxville when Uncle Gavin went in first, and Uncle Andy had to sit there and listen to the whole thing.

When it came to his turn, Uncle Andy couldn't do it because he had been listening to Uncle Gavin right before he had to go in.

"Dad gum," Uncle Andy said. "And for Big Munro to say that about his own son, you know something?"

"I bet we don't know the half of it," Aunt Adair said.

The adults were humoring each other so that I would get the message.

"Cruelty," my mother said. "Gavin says Clyne is cruel, and I believe him. Gavin says Munro told him he skins animals alive. Dear God in heaven. I can't bear any kind of torture."

I had already seen Clyne put my BB gun over the rabbit's eye less than an hour before.

Aunt Adair said, "I think Munro brings him to work because he's afraid to leave him alone. So he may come to work with his daddy, Rodney. Shaw knows never to go anywhere near Clyne."

"Just turn away," my mother said. "Walk in the other direction if you see him coming."

I thought about the rabbit sounding like two pieces of metal being scraped together and had to concentrate on the shiny little red rocking chair sitting beside the couch with the ceiling light reflecting off its polyurethane. Nana caught me looking at it and said,

"That was your mother's rocking chair when she was just a baby," Nana told me that every year.

Uncle Andy pointed at the chair and said: "We need to get

Munro in here tomorrow morning to put another coat of polyurethane on Rindy's chair. It's been at least a month, hasn't it?"

My mother put her hand on her face. "Andy. Dear God."

The den floor was polyurethaned as well as the stairs, the banisters, the basement steps, the upstairs hallway and the dining room. On one corner of the couch, where there was no carpeting, I liked to sit with bare feet and press my foot down into the polyurethane, lift it up and press it down, feeling it give way and stick to my toes.

Uncle Andy said, "Munro's scheduled to polyurethane the grandchildren this Saturday."

Uncle Gavin laughed, and Nana puffed out her cheeks. After that, no one spoke for a full minute until Nana broke the silence.

"Law. I think I'll have to get Marjorie in here to clean the portraits tomorrow."

A.F. Knott

5

MARJORIE, HI HO MAGNUS MATTHEWS AND CREAM OF WHEAT

Marjorie had been standing by the sink when I walked into the kitchen the next day. Her hair had turned full white since last summer. She whirled around, saw me and said: "Oh, Rodney!"

I sat and felt as I always had; if Marjorie was in a room, I didn't want to leave. She looked at me as if we shared a secret. I was never sure what our secret was but knew she wouldn't tell. Whenever I could, I liked to go with Nana in the Olds to pick up Marjorie or drop her off.

Before the sun set, I waited by the hallway window for Marjorie's taxi to come up the drive. I looked out the hallway window and felt sad when I saw the taxi sitting there. I went away, came back and when I looked again, the taxi had gone. Marjorie wasn't in the kitchen and the sun had almost gone down.

Every single time Nana gave Marjorie a ride, I rode in the Olds with her and crossed the train tracks. If there was a train, we had to wait. The trains that came through the town were a mile long with one black coal car after another after another.

Marjorie was married to a blind man named Cuffy who sat on the front porch of Marjorie's house whenever we pulled up. Marjorie and Cuffy lived on the one block where colored people lived and from the road at the top of the hill, you could look from one end of that block to the other and see all the houses at the same time. The middle of the road sagged, and all the houses tipped inward just a little as if they'd been laying at the bottom of a sack. The road came to an end at the foot of a steep brown hill. At the top of that hill was a tall Oak tree. My mother said they built that part of town exactly that way on purpose.

There used to be trouble in that part of town, Nana said, *but there hasn't been any for a while.*

My mother told me the trouble had come right after the Special Report two years ago came on announcing that Martin Luther King had just been assassinated in Tennessee by James Earl Ray. I remember that Special Report. They showed people pointing at the hotel balcony. You didn't see Martin Luther King shot but they showed the hotel balcony over and over and over.

When we drove down Marjorie's block, people were always sitting on their porches. We always stopped in front of Marjorie's house, and when Marjorie got onto her porch, Cuffy waved at us even though he was blind. Marjorie probably told Cuffy that Nana's car had pulled up, and that was when he waved. Maybe she told him just to wave. You could see Cuffy's teeth from the Olds. Cuffy always waved at us and smiled even though he couldn't see what we looked like or where we were.

When I asked Marjorie about her husband becoming blind, she never said a word. This was the only time she wouldn't answer one of my questions. Nana or my mother never answered me either. Marjorie's main job had been taking care of her husband since he had become blind.

Whenever we drove the Olds beside the railroad tracks to drop Marjorie off, the old locomotive engine and a coal car were always there, sitting by themselves on the extra set of tracks. After passing those two train cars, we turned the corner, went down the hill, drove the Olds to the end of the block, turned around and dropped Marjorie off. I always remembered which house was Marjorie's. It had a little bit of blue paint on one of its windows.

After Marjorie left in her cab, I went back upstairs and looked in my mother's room. She was sitting in front of her round mirror with the lights on staring at herself. I asked my mother about Cuffy again, and my mother said,

"Oh, I HOPE you didn't ask Marjorie that. Never ask Marjorie. It was so sad about what happened. Daddy said 'NEVER ask about Cuffy.' I remember one day asking Daddy to tell me about Marjorie's husband, and I called him Mr. Cleland." My mother imitated her daddy talking to her in a loud, angry voice. "'Don't you ever EVER say Mr. Cleland again. He's Cuffy.'"

My mother threw one hand up into the air. "Daddy never got angry. That's just the way it was with him and everybody. He was a good man, and I miss him so much, but I know he's in a good place. He appeared to me after he died and told me himself. NEVER tell anybody. I've never told this to anybody including Dad. This is a big tugger for me, BIG tugger."

My mother had changed the subject, from Cuffy to the ghost of her father. She had already told me many times not to say anything to anybody about seeing her daddy standing at the foot of her bed three days after he died and that he had smiled down on her so peacefully and told her that everything was going to be alright. She said she knew it was all going to be alright after that. I had already written the whole story down on my yellow pad two years before.

"I was seventeen years old when he died and loved him more than anything in the world. Mm mm."

I knew what was coming next. After every time my mother told me about her Daddy appearing she also told me the story of how Nana beat her under the covers every morning after her Daddy left for work.

"Daddy would get up at four o'clock every single morning of his life and go up to the coal mines. As soon as he left, Mother would come in with a switch, pull back the covers and beat me. Dixie slept in the same room and saw it happen every single morning. I asked Dixie, 'Did you remember that, Dixie?' 'Yes, I remember that,' she said."

Aunt Dixie played the organ at her church in North Carolina and was married to Uncle John, a minister. He was always working at his church and didn't come to Tennessee that much, like Dad.

Dixie was the good one, you see. Everything Dixie did was good. I was the rebel. Andy and I were more alike. Gavin worked like a horse. He did everything mother told him to do. Mother worked him to death.

My mother had told me all that before, and I had written it all down, so I just nodded when she said it all again.

Hanging on the den wall were pictures of Nana and my grandfather, my great grandfather and great grandmother. Each summer, when the adults gathered, they pointed to these portraits and spoke the same words they had spoken the summer before.

You should all know this. When great-granddaddy was ninety, he could get up from a chair without using his hands. He would get up just like this.

My mother got up from the couch without using her hands.

Ninety. He told us all that: Never use your hands to get up. That was one of the most important things you can do, he said; never to use your hands when getting up.

Uncle Andy raised his hand in the air like he was riding a bucking broncho.

Men, they called him Hi Ho Magnus Matthews.

Uncle Andy sometimes said *here come the men* instead of *here come the communists.* He called us *men* even if Lillian or the twins were with us.

My mother spoke in her deep voice and raised one hand into the air as if she was the Lone Ranger: *Hi Ho! Hi Ho Magnus Matthews!*

Uncle Andy raised his arm into the air as well.

Hi Ho Magnus Matthews. God, you know, he could walk into the middle of a group of angry miners all with their guns out, and they would listen to what he had to say. They respected him because he knew how to talk to people. He was good for his word, and they all knew that because he had been around so long and they heard all about him and knew what kind of man he was.

Everybody in the family knew the story of Hi Ho Magnus Matthews. Hi Ho had been an orphan. His real daddy had died when he was two months old. Hi Ho's mother married a coal miner then she died when Hi Ho was only three. Hi Ho's step-daddy raised him until he got drawn into coal rollers and crushed.

My mother turned her head and looked at the portraits. "Granddaddy's step-daddy was a bigger alcoholic than Perseus."

Nana said, "Oh, just hush. They had it so hard back then and settled in East Norwegian when Magnus was little. Magnus's step-daddy would leave for three or four days at a time and little Magnus would have to go out in the woods and eat tea leaves, birch bark, and slippery elm just to survive, Lord have mercy."

"Out in the woods by himself and just a little boy," my mother said. "Law."

My mother repeated words and sentences twice and spoke some words louder than others.

"He went to work in the mines when he was eight and eventually became a big success. Only three months of schooling his entire life. Three months and he saved every penny."

You have to know all these things, my mother always said.

I had heard every Magnus Matthews story more than five or six times: Hi Ho's step-daddy took him out to the bars when he was seven years old and made him fight the other miner's sons. Whichever miner's son won, that daddy received a pot of beer. Hi Ho won every single fight, and his step-daddy got one pot of beer after another.

My mother hated Hi Ho Magnus Matthews. Only Uncle Gavin, Dad and I knew how much she hated him.

'This will probably be Grandpa's last year with us so be very nice,' mother would say. Dear God, he lived for another fifteen. He had a thing about me, you see, and always wanted to take me on picnics. He had a mustache and was a very attractive looking man. Fit as a fiddle. It was awful. I didn't understand it at the time, you see. 'It'll probably be his last Christmas so be nice to your Grandpa Matthews.' Daddy named me after his wife, so Grandpa got us confused when he was old. 'My little Rindy Anne,' he'd say and be feeling me down there. I hated him, but I was stuck. I couldn't tell anybody.

~

Every morning, as soon as one of the cousins set foot in the kitchen, Nana told them:

Oh, Honey. Let me just dish you out a nice big bowl of this good Cream of Wheat right quick.

Nana stirred the Cream of Wheat on her stove for twenty minutes then *clacked* the wooden spoon against the side of our bowl when she was dishing it out.

Here comes your Cream of Wheat. And there's some of that good cold milk and brown sugar sitting right on the table for you.

Whenever Duncan stood in the middle of the driveway and yelled *Cream of Wheat* at the top of his lungs, I couldn't stop laughing. If we sat side by side at church and Duncan whispered *Cream of Wheat* into my ear, I'd have to hold my nose until I stopped shaking. If he whispered it a second time, I wouldn't be able to stand it, and my mother would end up making me cut my own switch after I got home from Bible School.

Cameron was still waiting for his cinnamon toast to come out of the oven by the time I finished my Cream of Wheat. The other cousins were still asleep. Cameron had planned on flying his balsa wood plane in the front yard after breakfast, but since I hadn't melted army men down in over eight months, I couldn't control my excitement. I snatched the box of kitchen matches out of the pantry and headed to the sandbox.

Munro leaned on his shovel by the front porch with the bill of his Sinclair cap flipped up. He pushed his cap a little farther back onto his head when he saw me. As soon as I got close to Munro, I smelled cigarettes and gasoline.

Nana didn't like Munro smoking his Winstons on the job so he sat on the little bench the other side of the big tulip tree in the front yard where he couldn't be seen from the house. Munro knew I wouldn't say anything, so he let me stand there and watch him smoke. Munro draped one leg over the other and placed the hand holding his Winston on top of the wrist laying on his knee. When Munro smoked, he pushed his filling station cap far back onto his head. I couldn't understand how it didn't fall off. After

Munro had fired his twenty-two, he smelled like a cap gun; if he had been working in Nana's basement, he smelled like oil on a chisel.

Last summer Munro had to pick up two new tires for Nana's Olds and I rode with him in his truck. On our way back, we spotted a tractor yanking up an old Oak. Munro pulled over to watch. With the windows rolled down, I took a deep breath at the moment the tree came up out of the ground with balls of dirt hanging off its roots swinging like sacks of potatoes. They all burst at the same time and dirt showered back into the hole. On days when Munro had been digging, he smelled exactly like those balls of dirt bursting.

"Can you walk alone?"

Munro asked me the same question every time he saw me, even before saying hello. Munro always looked like he was joking when he asked me that, and I never said anything because I didn't know how to answer his question. After he had asked me this time, I didn't say anything and made a beeline for the sandbox.

With two of my kneeling army men wedged into a mound of sand and three of them right below, I lit two rifles with one match and watched black smoke begin to pour off as drop after drop of flaming plastic fell. The three below caught fire and began to smoke as well.

As soon as I saw Clyne and the boy with red hair step out of the woods, I stood up but couldn't move. Clyne said,

"Those green men aren't real."

I knew my green army men weren't real and wondered

why Clyne had gone to the trouble of saying that. I didn't know what to say so I said,

"I know karate."

Clyne looked interested and said,

"I know damn judo."

"What?" I said.

"I'm joining the real army and know about that damn karate as well but lookie here."

Clyne took my arm and pulled me over the top of his shoulder into a flip. The ground knocked the wind out of me, and I had been trying to breathe when Clyne turned to the other boy.

"Come over, Red. I need practicing my hand to hand before they put those goddamn sergeant's stripes on my sleeve. They said they'd be making me sergeant as soon as I set foot through the goddamn door."

"Hain't moving," Red said.

"I know you hain't and know why. I saw you standing alongside Kezia Willoughby and I know you saw me watching her whisper in those big ears of yours. Now I've got my Supreme Court witness." Clyne nodded toward me. Clyne didn't know what I knew; that everybody called Kezia Willoughby *the town pump*.

"Reach me one of those burning army men," Clyne told me. I couldn't move.

Clyne took one of Red's arms, twisted it then pulled the

boy down by the side of the sandbox. I started getting dizzy when Clyne put his boot on Red's arm then put his knee on his neck.

"Hold still."

I still couldn't move. Clyne reached down and picked up one of my burning snipers and pushed its gun, with a drop of hot plastic dangling off of it, all the way down into Red's ear. Red turned over like the rabbit in the front yard had and vomited into the sandbox then rolled over onto his back.

I couldn't hold my head up after that. Clyne pushed that side of Red's head down against the sand, picked up my other burning army man and jammed that one into Red's other ear as far as it would go then pushed in further with the bottom of his shoe. He took his knee off Red and watched him.

Red yanked both Army men out of his ears. Something came out on one side that made a noise like twigs crackling in a fire. A red string trailed behind with little white pieces of shell sticking to it. Red vomited a second time then fell onto his back holding both ears.

"They call that a hear-no-evil," Clyne said.

I still lay on the ground after the flip and had to roll out of the boy's way as he fell. Red rose to his feet after that. His eyes were jerking from side to side and he held his hands out in front of him as if he were blind. Red fell over again, this time sideways, and hit his head on the corner of the sandbox, sounding like a watermelon had been cracked open. He lay there and didn't move. Blood and sand caked one ear with my melted green army men sticking to his neck. Clyne pointed at me.

"You're my Supreme Court Witness. That's what hear-no-evil looks like. If it's a see-no, I'll take his eyes. If it's a speak-no, I'll pull out the man's tongue with pliers or burn it off. Over in Viet Nam, a man uses what comes into his reach. Your army men came into mine, so that makes you my accessory. If you tell anybody what you saw, that'll be a see-no, and I'll take your eyes out, then come back and take out your granny and momma's eyes."

Clyne wasn't just *off*; he was *way off*. Dad would have called what Clyne just said *complete shit*.

Uncle Andy already told us that the Army wouldn't take Clyne, but Clyne had just said the Army was making him a Sergeant. He told me I was accessory to the crime and his Supreme Court Witness. Red wasn't moving a muscle. I had to put my head down and couldn't see anything but darkness between the trees. The sky was getting darker around me. It had been clear blue a second before.

"His ears needed minding their own business, so he got the hear-no-evil."

Clyne took Red by one arm, yanked his body around then began dragging him past the swing set into the woods toward the greenhouse. I stood in the sandbox listening to the leaves rub against Clyne and the sticks crack under Red. Trees swayed back and forth as they moved through the woods then stopped. Clyne cursed. There was a bigger *crash,* then a *crack.* Branches shook. Red's body had got caught on something. I stood and listened to the sticks cracking until I couldn't hear them any longer.

Cameron had seen the flip and had run back into the

house to tell Nana. He hadn't seen what Clyne had done to Red, though. Only I had seen that.

"Did Clyne flip you?" My mother asked when I came into the kitchen.

"He was showing me judo. The flip wasn't bad."

"Oh, he knew EXACLTY what he was doing." my mother said.

6

THE MAN FROM THE CLOSET, LIGHT THROUGH YONDER WINDOW, AND THE MAN WITH THE GOLDEN ARM, ALL VISIT IN ONE NIGHT

That night, *the man from the closet* appeared. He came every summer but never this early. I never mentioned him to either my mother, Nana or the cousins because I was worried that if I did, the man might not come back. He never once made a sound or tried to scare me but would stare at the ceiling as if holding back a grin and looked as though he was glad to be laying on top of a nice bed. He might have been a little worried somebody would come and tell him to take his feet off the covers.

There had never been any warnings before the man showed up. If there had, I missed them. I'd turn my head and there he'd be, laying stock still, dressed in the same gray work shirt buttoned to the collar along with his same brown work pants and same black shoes, their laces tied in bows. The man held his hands straight down by his side as if standing at attention.

I never thought the man's coming had been a dream. He never showed up late, and when he did, either the hall light or the light from my mother's room was on and shining into my room.

I assumed the man was a ghost and searched all of Nana's photographs of town's people which she kept in the den drawer but never spotted him. I called him *the man from the closet* because the closet door was always cracked open on nights he came; and he always lay on the window side of my bed, right beside that door. The long cedar closet behind the bed ran all the way to the bathroom wall. There was plenty of room in there for him to stay.

Every time the man came, I was filled with disbelief. As a test, I looked away then looked back and the man was always there, moving his mouth, but just barely, as if to say: *I have passed the test.* I couldn't be sure that's what he was thinking.

I studied a different part of his clothing with each visit. Last summer I had examined the collar and the top of his shirt where it buttoned right underneath the chin. His shirt may have been red but only gray threads folded over around his neck. His button dangled by four threads and would fall off if he even tried to button it one more time.

This summer, I examined his shoes: Dried mud caked their bottoms and splattered the leather which was the opposite of shiny. His laces were tied in bows; one lace was brown, the other black.

The man did something different. He turned his head and stared at me right in the eyes as if he had been thinking about something mischievous. Even though he stared at me like that, I could tell the man wasn't planning on doing anything drastic. After a few minutes though, I couldn't be sure what his plans were or why he had turned his head to look at me this time when he hadn't done that in all the other times he visited before. Without taking my eyes off the man from the closet, I climbed out of bed and walked backward, step by step, into the hallway. I turned to have a look into my mother's room, saw her foot on the edge of the bed then turned back. My bed was empty. The man from the closet had left.

I didn't think the man would be able to protect me from Clyne but something told me he already knew about the hear-no-evil. Laying back down, I stared at the ceiling and imagined the ghost of my grandfather standing at the foot of my mother's bed. I remembered everything she had told me.

Don't tell anybody I told you this or they might think I was crazy but I believe it was him. I was as wide awake as I am now.

The first time my mother said she had come straight out and said she had seen the ghost of her daddy standing at the foot of her bed, I stopped playing and listened more closely than I usually did to what she was saying.

Everything was alright after I saw daddy standing there. He told me, 'Everything is going to be OK, Monnie.' I knew that he would be with mother and me after that, watching over us.

My mother was convinced she had seen her daddy. I could not be sure that her story was true. I did not think my mother was a crazy person but wished that she had not told me she had seen a ghost or that I was the only one in the world she could tell. Looking at the spot at the foot of her bed where she pointed, I asked,

Right there?

Yes, right there. You can't tell anybody. If you say something like that, some people will think you are crazy, so it's best not to say

anything to ANYBODY. But he was dressed in his favorite robe and smoking his favorite pipe. I recognized the pipe. He looked down at me and said, 'Don't worry Monnie, it's all going to be ok.'

The ghost of her daddy called my mother by her nickname Monnie. I asked her if it could all have been a dream as she had been laying on her bed when he appeared.

Oh no, it was him. He protects me and protects you and looks down over all of us. He watches over mother.

Even though I had never been afraid of the man from the closet, if he had suddenly appeared at the foot of my bed as my grandfather had to my mother, I might have jumped or screamed.

Did you jump or scream when he appeared?

Oh no. I felt no fear at all. He was surrounded by the most beautiful light you could ever imagine in your life, and he looked as peaceful as I had ever seen him. He was wearing his favorite robe.

Every time my mother told me the story of her daddy appearing, she always added that he had been wearing his favorite robe. One time she said he was smoking his favorite pipe.

Jesus came out of his tomb on the third day, and his disciples had seen him walking around for a little while after that. Doubting Thomas did not believe it was him until he stuck a finger through the hole in Jesus' hand. After that, Jesus disappeared and didn't come back. Perhaps my grandfather had left his coffin on the third day, like Jesus had, came back to Nana's house and visited both my mother and Nana before going up.

Finding Jesus' tomb empty was the most mysterious part of the story. The part when they saw him walking around later was less interesting. I felt sad when Jesus disappeared for the last time. His disciples had grown used to him, going out on their missions and hearing his speeches.

Mr. Barnes, the Bible School teacher, said Jesus' story wasn't sad but joyous. He said it was difficult for children to understand why the story was joyous. He was right. I didn't understand why it was joyous. I asked my mother,

Did you ever see your daddy after that?

Yes, I did. He must have gone down the hallway before he went up. I saw him standing at the end of the hallway looking down on Mother. Then that was it.

When Shirley Temple's family friend took her up in his airplane, he pointed to the clouds outside the cockpit window and told her it was heaven.

We're right in it now. It's all around us. Every place you look.

I wished more than anything in the world that Shirley's parents had been standing on the clouds holding hands and waving at her, but there had been no one outside the cockpit window. In the same movie, Shirley sang Good Ship Lollipop and skipped down the airplane aisle while her daddy's pilot friends sat in the passenger seats, got up one by one and hit her in the face with cakes and pies. I thought it odd that Shirley kept skipping and shaking her curls after getting hit. Nana told me:

After you die, you see everybody you've ever know up in heaven and live with them forever.

My mother said *They'll be dressed like they were when they were at their happiest, in their favorite bathrobe or bathing suit.*

Dad said *Heaven is utter shit.*

Dad hates church, you see. Hates it. It all backfired because Gran and Grandad were missionaries. Too much religion. They used to hold hands and sing all day long. All that was too much for Dad. They sent him to boarding school when he was seven. It all backfired.

Dad frequently used the Lord's name in vain.

Dad isn't the only one. We all do it.

My mother laughed whenever Dad cursed because Dad cursed with his English accent. I wrote down all of Dad's curses and practiced saying them out loud:

Bugger Fuck Shit. Look at all this godawful, complete and utter shit.

~

After the man from the closet's visit, I fell asleep and was woken by my mother shrieking at the top of her lungs. My mother never shrieked at the top of her lungs in Tennessee because the street light across the driveway drew a glowing white line along my floor, out the door, crossing the hallway to shine on her opposite wall and reflect off all the mirrors in her room. This white line kept darkness out as long as her door was open.

Uncle Andy knew about my mother's bad dreams, and

would sometimes watch her closely then say:

What light through yonder window breaks?

That night my mother had closed her door and forgot to open the blinds.

Mother used to lock me in the upstairs closet and wouldn't let me out, so I've had the same dream every night since I was a little girl. I'm in a room with no light and no windows, and I can't find a way out. I'm trying to find the window to let light in, you see. I'm ok as long as I can find the light.

In New York, my mother sleep-walked across our apartment and into my room to touch the blinds on my window then start clawing at them if she couldn't find enough light. I put the pillow over my head when I heard clawing because I knew after clawing came screaming. My mother screamed as if she was being stabbed to death in *Bird with the Crystal Plumage*.

If it had been a bad week up in New York, I slept under my bed because my room didn't have a door. I tried not to pay attention to what she was doing but sometimes the police came to investigate, and I would have to get up and answer questions. The neighbors always thought my mother was being knifed to death and stood in the hallway craning their necks.

I watched Chiller Theater with my mother every Friday night in New York. Most of the time the movie playing wasn't too scary, and I could stand it. It was nowhere near as bad as clawing at the blinds. One Friday they showed *House on Haunted Hill* while Dad was visiting the apartment. He sat down on the living room couch, said *interesting*, then got up and didn't come back. *House on Haunted Hill* showed a face which I recognized from my nightmares, so I got up and didn't come back either. Dad was already in the bathroom, so I went into the kitchen, opened the refrigerator, pulled off a handful of raw hamburger, sprinkled salt on and ate it.

I wish I had never seen *Bird with the Crystal Plumage*. Dad had wanted to go so I went with him and was glad he sat beside me. He had been interested in the plot twist but not all that interested. I wasn't interested at all in the plot twist and didn't like seeing the murderer standing in the doorway dressed in shiny black clothing. When Dad guessed that the killer had been a woman, he got up and went to the bathroom. He came back right before the end and whispered to me about how good his Raisenettes tasted. If Dad figured out the plot to a movie, he got up, went to the bathroom and didn't come back.

~

After my mother stopped shrieking, all the lights were turned on. Uncle Andy and Uncle Gavin finally went back downstairs, my mother came into my room and began talking. After a nightmare, she took a few minutes to begin speaking slowly.

"I started wheezing again. I never wheezed after leaving home, never. I think it's the polyurethane; that's what I think. I would wheeze all night long after she polyurethaned. As soon as I left home, I never wheezed."

After my mother calmed down and returned to her room,

Shaw and the twins, Hilda and Tilda, came in and stood beside my bed.

"Nana told Munro that you said Clyne flipped you," Shaw said.

"Cameron said that. I didn't say that."

"Munro beat Clyne with an iron skillet after he was told on. Clyne told everybody in town that he's coming after you."

"I didn't tell on Clyne."

After Shaw told me that, I lay there wishing more than anything in the world I had waited with Cameron for his cinnamon toast to come out of the oven then went with him into the front yard and watch his balsa wood plane fly. Instead, I had gone out to the sandbox by myself and burned my little green army men. If I hadn't done that, I wouldn't have seen anything and wouldn't be feeling like the woman in *Crowhaven Farm*. When the cousins watched *Crowhaven Farm* in Nana's room this week, I had to slip out of the room when the Puritans started piling stones on top of her until she confessed. The woman turned in her husband.

Shaw looked at the twins then said, "Rindy was telling us the polyurethane was making her wheeze. But did you know the man with the golden arm likes polyurethane because polyurethane muffles his approaching footsteps."

Hilda said, "The man with the golden arm climbed out of his grave tonight and asked,

Who's got my golden arm?

He stood beside his tombstone then step by step, walked through the cemetery gates. Step by step, he followed the railroad tracks all the way through town, knowing which direction he needed to go. He stopped in front of Rexall and asked,

Who's got my golden arm?

Step by step, he crossed Main Street and started up Tennessee Avenue."

Tilda said, "There are footsteps in the driveway, and the gravel crunches with every step he takes."

Who's got my golden arm? Both twins spoke at the same time.

Tilda said, "He is standing right outside Nana's house, and you can hear his foot scuffing when he steps up onto the porch. When he opens the front door, it *creeeeeaks*. In the hallway, the man's shoes barely squeak on Nana's polyurethane, but you can still hear him taking every single slow step, one by one. His squeaking footsteps get louder and louder and louder on Nana's polyurethane because he's careful to walk right beside the carpet while he's in the second-floor hallway."

Who's got my golden arm? Shaw, Hilda, and Tilda all spoke at the same time.

"His shoes squeaked ever so slightly on the polyurethane outside your room," Tilda said.

Who's got my golden arm? They all asked.

The lights from my mother's room cut across the hall and shined behind and all around the man as he stood in the doorway. I couldn't see his face, but I could see his arm was missing.

Who's got my golden arm? They all asked.

Hilda said, "He's standing on top of the thick polyurethane right beside your bed, the light behind him so that his face and everything about him stays in the shadows."

The floor of my room, covered in thick, shiny polyurethane, was as soft as the polyurethaned cedar chest under my window or the polyurethaned banister at the top of the stairs or the polyurethaned den floor.

The man hadn't been afraid to come straight through Nana's front door and walk up the stairs, even with all the lights on. He stood by my bed and didn't say a word, just stood there until his good arm lunged out, grabbed a hold of me and shouted:

IT WAS YOU THAT GOT MY GOLDEN ARM!

I jumped out of bed and screamed at the top of my lungs. The twins and Shaw laughed. All three of them had grabbed me and shouted at the same time. Even though I'd heard the whole story before, I still jumped. Whoever was telling the story knew what was going to happen and whoever was listening imagined the Man with the Golden Arm coming and coming and coming and coming. I jumped way up and flinched every time his hand grabbed mine because I had listened so carefully how he had made his way closer and closer, step by step.

I went back to sleep after they all left and found myself walking through the same room as I had the night before. I knew the incarnation of Evil was lurking in the hallway on the other side of the wall and recognized the same furniture covered in white sheets.

I used the Lord's Prayer right off the bat to prevent the incarnation of Evil from reaching out and touching me: *Our Father, who art in Heaven, hallowed be thy name, thy kingdom come, they will be done.*

The louder I spoke the Lord's Prayer, the farther away the incarnation stayed. I couldn't run when the incarnation was in the room but wondered while I was in my dream if the incarnation might not be able to touch me. I couldn't imagine the incarnation of Evil touching me. As soon as Evil touched me, it would be all over. I kept the incarnation at bay with the Lord's Prayer and examined the white sheets covering the furniture, then looked back at the doorway, knowing Evil was coming in at any moment. I was able to walk, but I didn't look back. The incarnation of Evil was in the room with me and made a sound, like scratching. I didn't turn because I couldn't move my head but continued to recite the Lord's Prayer. Evil didn't want to touch me after that and everything became quiet, still and dark.

I walked into the next room and couldn't be sure that Evil hadn't followed me and wasn't lurking behind the couch. I didn't look behind the couch and kept walking through room after room, all of them with white sheets covering the chairs. The incarnation of Evil was always three steps behind. I needed something more to fight it with, so in the last room I arrived in, I took possession of a gun, turned, saw something, and shot. It turned out I had shot the incarnation itself, hitting it right in the arm. It felt good shooting the incarnation. It flinched. Instead of reciting the Lord's Prayer, I spoke in a loud voice like John Wayne:

You son of a bitch!

Shooting the gun into the incarnation of Evil felt as good as flying above the trees did in other dreams. I couldn't kill Evil but liked shooting it. Evil disappeared for a second or two after being shot then came back, reached out and took the gun out of my hand.

The incarnation of Evil always turned the tables as soon as I did something. I moved faster and stepped out onto a balcony. I knew the incarnation was coming out onto the balcony, had my gun and wouldn't hesitate to shoot me, so I lowered myself over the side of the railing and moved along the outside of the building like a flying squirrel.

I forgot about the incarnation of Evil, didn't know if it was following any longer and didn't care because I found myself running along the outside wall as well as bouncing and liked how that felt. Bouncing was almost as good as flying because I wasn't falling. As soon as I thought about falling, I began dropping straight down like a brick and didn't have time to be more scared than I ever had been in my life because the dream ended as soon as I dropped. I was just glad my eyes opened.

I studied the polyurethane hills and polyurethane waves on top of the window chest then looked out at the streetlight pole on the other side of Nana's driveway. I craned my neck to examine the sundial and the bees flying around it then climbed out of bed and walked into the hall. My mother was sitting in front of her makeup table looking into her round mirror with the lights surrounding it. Adair sat in the chair by the door.

In New York, my mother kept the same mirror on the

makeup table in the middle of her closet. She was an actress, so her closet had long mirrors on every wall. My mother tried on dress after dress after dress, came out into the living room and asked which one was the best. I had Matchbox and Hot Wheels races on top of the living room couch going on every single night, so I answered when I could. Dad didn't usually stay over, so I was the judge, looked quick and picked quick. I was able to glance up, say *that one*, and she would say *I think you're right* then go back into her closet to another while I kept racing.

I went into the bathroom, sat on the pot and tried not to let my snake splash in the bowl so I could hear every word of what my mother and Adair were saying.

"I rebelled, you see. I loved makeup and loved to dress up," my mother told Adair. She always said *you see* when she explained her rebelling. My mother had told me all her rebellion stories before so I stopped paying attention. I looked at the toilet paper roll then at the sink. My mother began talking louder though, so I had no choice but to listen.

"That's how I survived, Adair. Mother would say, 'I'll switch you,' but I would sneak downstairs anyway and put makeup on before school." My mother imitated Nana. "'She's down there with her cascara putting it all over her face.' Mother called it cascara. She would beat me every time I put mascara on. Anything I did wasn't good enough. Mother told me, 'You're going to be sweeping cobwebs out of a miner's shack.'"

Adair started laughing.

My mother said, "But I rebelled, you see, and put mascara

64

on every chance I got. I just loved makeup. 'She's down there with her cascara,'" my mother said again. Adair kept laughing and laughing.

My mother loved to put Nivea cream all over her face. Dad and I both hated Nivea cream. My mother got it all over the faucets and tape recorders and water glasses. Dad slept at his own apartment because of that. I lived in my room. Nivea cream made me shiver whenever I saw it on the bathroom faucet.

When she was seventeen, my mother ran away to New York to become an actress after her daddy died. One of the first things they taught her in acting school was how to put on makeup.

Uncle Andy said *Big New York* in the same way as he said *Big Perseus* or *Hi Ho Magnus Matthews*.

If the adults were sitting in the den without talking, Uncle Andy might say *It's a big deal up there in New York.* After that, he wouldn't say anything, or he might just say, *Lynden Baines Johnson* or *Malcolm X* or *J. Edgar Hoover* then nothing else.

7

THE GARDEN, THE WILLOUGHBY SISTERS, AND THE STATE TROOPER

The next day Duncan and I went into the garden to investigate the tadpole pond where Old May told Nana she had seen Clyne busting Kezia Willoughby. The tadpole pond used to be called *Tinker Bell's Fountain* in the days when the garden was a showcase. Nana still called it that. Tinker Bell had been the first character to be shot.

She used to hold a wand in one hand and be poised on a beautiful glass pedestal as if she had been listening.

No one knew where Tinker Bell's body had gone. Only a rusty pipe stuck straight out of the water where her pedestal once stood.

When Daddy was alive, Tinker Bell's Fountain was THE big attraction.

The tadpole pond became thick, green and brown. Leaves fell onto the surface then sank. The pond had no tadpoles, only water skeeters, and they did nothing but stay still. The tadpole pond was about as wide as Nana's kitchen table, but we still called it a pond.

Duncan checked for footprints around the trees where Old May might have been lurking. I checked the pond. The mayflies dabbed at me, so I had to keep one hand waving back and forth in front of my face and couldn't see much because of that.

I lifted myself up onto the stone wall and focused my eyes straight down, like looking into a dirty glass case. Last summer I could see all the leaves sitting on the bottom of the pond and they reminded me of pages from an old book, all of them carefully stacked. This year, the sticks had been shoved over to one side of the pond with everything stirred up and I wondered if Munro had been working on the tadpole pond that week. I took a big branch that lay on top of the wall and pushed it into the water all the way to the bottom. The stick snagged on something and I had to jerk it at first then yank it. A green army man with a half-melted body came twirling up. As soon as I saw that, I knew exactly which army man it was. The melted army man twisted away and sank into the churning cloud.

Twigs cracked under Duncan's feet, and I jumped. While he kept looking behind one of the trees, I pushed the branch down like a shovel and hit something big. A smooth white leg came drifting up out of the water on the other side of the pond. I let go of the stick and the leg dropped back down. In the middle of the swirl below me, the boy's red hair twisted around and around before dirt and leaves closed back in over it. I left the stick in the middle of the pond, climbed down from the wall and walked over to watch Duncan examine the ground beside the gazebo.

"She may have been standing right here. There's a print."

I looked at the spot and nodded but couldn't see anything. Everything blurred, and I had to keep my hands on both knees otherwise I would fall over. While bent over looking where Duncan was pointing, I saw the red-haired boy's leg coming up out of the water again, moving ever so slowly.

The leg had taken a long time to settle back down below the surface of the tadpole pond and I thought for a second it never would. Duncan pointed at the spot while I kept nodding and holding onto the side of the gazebo with one hand to keep from toppling over. The darkness between the trees was getting darker. I was accessory to the crime and Clyne's Supreme Court witness.

"Did you find anything?" Duncan asked.

"No."

"Let's see if we can figure out the dwarves."

I followed Duncan over to the Ivy away from the tadpole pond but had to stop and lean over and shut my eyes. The trees were spinning around me as if they were ballerinas.

After Nana had stopped taking care of the garden, people drove up and down the Florist Shop Road and shot at the dwarves with their twenty-twos. Snow White had been blown off her pedestal with a shotgun and lay slumped in the cat grass. There were two wires sticking out where her arms had been; Shaw said dogs had torn them off. The cousins never went into the cat grass to take a look at Snow White because a big black snake lived on that side of the garden. Munro told me he saw it stretched out all the way across the Florist Shop Road, sunning itself and tried to run it over.

The thing moved as fast as a stream of water.

I never paid attention to the old white log in the cat grass until I saw the picture of Snow White holding up her lantern in the sun. In the Den cabinet, Nana kept three photographs of the garden taken before I was born. That was one of them. After seeing Snow White with her lantern, every single time I made my way down the garden steps, I craned my neck to catch a glimpse of her. Once you were at the bottom of the steps, the cat grass was too high to see anything.

Most of the dwarves were nothing but rotten nubs. Sleepy was the only dwarf who had kept his face. Grumpy's head had been split down the middle. Shaw said it would have taken more than a twenty-two to have knocked him over. Sneezy's body was left turned sideways in the Ivy, and we only knew it to be him because somebody had written *Sneezy* on the bottom of his pedestal.

One dwarf was still standing. The cousins didn't know for sure which one he had been. Shaw said they had left this particular dwarf standing because you couldn't see him from the road after he had been shot. All that was left of his head was a nubbin with one eye sitting on top of a splinter. The eye was turned down and looked sadder the closer you got.

Because the dark garden looked so different from the showcase garden, I didn't believe they were the same and opened the den drawer to look at the three photographs every chance I got. I opened the den drawer as often as I opened the first-floor bathroom drawer to look at Nana's tube. In the first picture, all Seven Dwarves were lined up in a row, the sun was shining and Snow White, with her black hair and blue dress, held up her lantern.

It had been the most beautiful blue dress in the world.

In the second picture, the gazebo sat in full sunlight with no trees hanging over it, and no brown leaves on its roof or moss on its shingles. The water spraying out of Tinker Bell's Fountain twinkled, with bright sun shining down on everything.

In the third picture, my mother stood by a car parked in the sunshine on the Florist Shop Road. She said Nana had made her ticket taker the day the photograph was taken and she thought the people in the car had driven all the way from Ohio.

The garden was considered one of the biggest showcases in East Tennessee.

~

That Sunday we were all climbing into the Olds to go to church when my mother said:

"It's just so sad about that little red-haired boy who came to work with Clyne the day he flipped you. He was just supposed to help Munro pull up one of mother's dead pines, but Clyne is saying he just walked off. The Sheriff doesn't believe Clyne."

As we pulled down the driveway, I looked out the window at the red dogwood seeds on the green branches and blurred my eyes: The dogwoods had been shot and were all standing there bleeding to death.

Nana pulled over to give the three Willoughby sisters a ride. If Nana didn't give them a ride, the Willoughbys walked the four miles into town to get to church. As we drove closer, the sisters looked like they were tied together by two ropes: The front rope pulled tight while the back rope went slack with every few steps. I was afraid they were going to run into each other but they didn't.

Whenever we spotted the Willoughby sisters, I rolled down my window as fast as I could. If I had forgotten to roll down my window and the sisters got into the car, I would vomit into my mouth. If the sisters got into the car and I hadn't rolled my window down in time, Nana wouldn't let me do it. She said it was rude to do that if they were already in the car.

Nana didn't care if the Willoughbys were inside the car and the windows were rolled up at the same time. Nana could drink a full glass of sour milk standing in front of me, and if she poured a glass of sour milk and I didn't drink it, she'd say,

Ok then, it'll be waiting for you in the refrigerator. It didn't matter if it had turned or not in my day, you had to drink your milk.

If I forgot to drink the sour milk waiting for me in the refrigerator, Nana put the glass next to my Cream of Wheat the following morning. I would have to tell my mother what Nana had done. My mother would sneak downstairs after Nana went to bed and pour it down the sink then say the next morning that she had drunk it by mistake.

With the three sisters sitting in the back seat of the Olds, I breathed in and out very slowly through my mouth. All three had their hair combed flat against the side of their head looking like they'd been camping in the Smokies. I had heard every single Willoughby sister story five or ten times over.

They don't wash.

No, I don't think they do.

I don't even notice. Those poor sisters don't even have electric or have a car. They're so poor; they have to haul their water from the well at the bottom of our hill.

Law mother, I remember we stopped using that well after Daddy found the nest of rattlesnakes at the bottom. That must have been years and years ago. We used to think the spring water was the best in the world.

'Isn't it wonderful,' Daddy would say. We had our own spring, you see, and that was a big deal. But we didn't know that there were rattlesnakes living down there.

'Have you ever tasted better water in your entire life?' Daddy used to say.

'Have some of this good cold water,' Mother would say. I don't know how much the rattlesnakes contributed to the taste, but they must have, to some extent.

I don't think there were ever any rattlesnakes in our well, Rindy Anne.

Mother, there were. Big ones. You made Gavin climb down there and get them out.

The cousins called the older Willoughby sister Lurch. Her real name was Jemima. The second oldest was Kezia, the one Clyne liked; the youngest was Stib. Job Willoughby, their father, died when Jemima was twenty-one and their mother died when they were all little.

The poor things never really knew their mother. Job Willoughby would beat them right on the church steps. They say he may have done other things to them we don't know about. He was friends with my Daddy though and laid the foundation of our house and helped Daddy carry the stones down from the mountains. Job Willoughby built the two cedar closets in your room.

Mr. Willoughby never once allowed the three sisters to leave their house unless he had been with them. After he died, Lurch didn't let the younger two leave either. She took them to town twice a week, once on Tuesday and once on Sunday Morning. They all attended the First Baptist Church where Nana played the organ.

Whenever we drove out onto the Loop, I craned my neck and tried to find the Willoughby sisters house through the trees but only saw dark woods in the direction Nana pointed, like searching the hill behind the Florist Shop for Perseus' house.

They say Job Willoughby's body disappeared into thin air. His daughters never arranged a funeral service at Maggot's, and he was never buried at the cemetery.

My cousin Brody, who was in medical school at UT said: *Job Willoughby died down in the mines breathing a combination of carbon monoxide and laughing gas that forms after an explosion.*

He was still smiling they said when they found him in the mine shaft.

The three sisters put his body in a burlap bag, carried it off the mountain and all the way across town to their house without stopping. No one heard anything about him after that.

The sisters couldn't afford a service, poor old things.

That's just so odd. Everybody has some kind of remembrance. Some people will bury their own in the backyard, but even then, there are usually words spoken. I told Shaw I didn't want him going anywhere near that house.

But that's how those people are. A lot of them don't involve the police if there's a crime up in the mountains, even bad ones. They won't talk about it.

Aunt Adair already knew the biggest Daredevil Club dare of all time was going up the hill behind the gazebo and touching the Willoughby's house. Shaw had already told the cousins at our summer meeting that the Willoughby sisters kept a hog pen at the top of their hill and that he had seen it from a distance when he was half way up but had never been to the top where the woods ended.

Jemima Willoughby doesn't allow anybody but May Tarwater on her property.

If you start at the gazebo and keep walking straight up the hill, you'll run right smack into their hog pen where the trees end. For the dare to count, you have to look the hog in the eye, touch its pen then go over and touch their house.

The adults didn't want the cousins going anywhere near the Willoughby house.

Lawsie. Jemima Willoughby keeps a shotgun by her door, and she'll use it. Some people think that there might be a few people buried up there in their yard, people who have disappeared from the town. Even the Sheriff is afraid to go up there.

Munro told us that the Willoughby hog guarded the gates of hell, and didn't let anybody come into his pen that wasn't already going to hell. Perseus told us that the hog was dangerous and if one of us was stupid enough to get caught in its pen, not to look at it in the eye. That's why Shaw told us that looking at it in the eye was part of the dare.

Munro told me Job Willoughby had been humping Lurch when he was still alive.

Dear GOD Andy! Poor old thing. That's why she looks the way that she does.

I think both Munro and Perseus have humped her.

Law, Andy!

Jemima Willoughby was taller than either of her two sisters by a foot and had a face like the Adams family butler, Lurch. Uncle Gavin thought Jemima had a brain tumor and told her she could get help in Nashville. Lurch refused to go and kept growing. Every time Duncan saw Lurch, he whispered,

You rang?

"Well I'll say, what pretty yellow dresses," Nana said as soon as the Willoughby sisters got in the car.

I turned around to say hello but didn't know what to say after that because all three Willoughbys were looking straight ahead.

The two younger sisters never talked, not even a hello or a thank you. Lurch sometimes spoke about the commandments and sometimes bossed the other two, but during most of the rides, all three sat still the whole ride to church and didn't say one word.

Once the sisters were sitting in the car, and the doors were closed, out of the corner of my eye I couldn't help but peek up into the rear-view mirror. I didn't turn my head but allowed my eyes to float up, and was unable to stop myself from looking at either Lurch's big head with the bow on top or Kezia's shelf of teeth. I had to yank the corner of my eye away after I did.

Just pretend that you don't see anything.

The middle sister's teeth stuck straight out like a soap dish even when her mouth was closed. I wanted to get right in front of Kezia and look at her teeth while she stayed still.

Nana said, *When you see the Willoughbys, always compliment them on their yellow dresses. They're so poor; that's all they have to wear.*

I couldn't complement the Willoughbys, but Nana and my mother did.

My, what pretty yellow dresses.

Duncan yelled out: *My, what pretty yellow dresses, what pretty yellow dresses, what pretty yellow dresses.*

When the Willoughby sisters got in the car this time, the younger one, Stib, began to cry. Lurch didn't say anything for a full minute then slapped Stib across the face. The younger sister stopped crying after that and sat still in her yellow church dress.

The big one constantly beats Kezia. I saw Jemima at the post office yanking her up from the ground by her hair. Munro saw her do worse and told mother but mother didn't pay any attention.

'It's not our business. We don't know what she did to deserve that.'

I know why. Kezia is having sex with Clyne every chance she can get because she's REBELLING. It's just all so normal.

The three sisters wore the same yellow dresses every week to church and Lurch wore the same yellow bow, big enough to hang on the front door, and almost as big as a Christmas wreath.

There's the bow! Just look at it. Look at the bow, Rodney.

Duncan talked to me about the bow when we were sitting side by side in church. When he did that, I held my nose until my ears popped.

Whenever Lurch was sitting in church, I squinted until all I saw in front of me was a blur. I directed my eyes toward the back of everybody's head in the congregation and moved them back and forth. When I saw a bright yellow light, I opened my eyes. Duncan said, *Behold, the bow.*

Nana always told Lurch, *Well, I'll say, what a pretty yellow bow you're wearing.*

If we were already seated and the sisters came in late, they rushed down the aisle looking like yellow flowers blown in by a gust of wind. Their smell came in afterward, like a pack of dogs that didn't bark. Everybody in the congregation looked straight ahead at the minister and breathed through their mouths like I had to do in the Olds.

Smelling the Willoughby sisters was a part of going to church, as was looking straight ahead as if there was no smell at all.

~

The Tennessee State Trooper's car sat in the driveway right in front of the steps when we pulled up in the Olds after Bible School.

"Oh, there he is," my mother said. I could tell my mother had already known that the State Trooper was going to be there.

"I think Aunt Adair said she needed to speak to you about something in the kitchen. I don't know what it's about just that she wanted to speak to you. I wonder what that police car is doing here. Mother do you know anything about that?"

My mother was pretending. We all went into the kitchen where the Tennessee State Trooper was standing beside Nana's stove, holding his hat in front of him.

"Here he is. Rodney, this is Deputy Rogers. Honey, I'll tell you the truth. I called him over because you may be the last person to see that boy that came with Clyne on the morning he flipped you over his shoulder."

The Tennessee State Trooper said, "This shouldn't take too long. We figure you probably didn't see anything Rodney but even if we know which direction those two boys went that may help us out. We're trying to find out as much as we can. You did see a boy with red hair that morning with Clyne? Your cousin said they had both been standing out there by your sandbox."

"Yes, just tell him. Tell what you saw."

"Yes, they were both there."

"Did anything happen while you were out in the sandbox?"

"I got flipped, but I didn't mind the flip."

"That's what I heard. I also heard you study karate up there in New York. And Clyne told you he knew judo. Was that it?"

"Yes."

"Did Clyne do anything to the other boy while you were there with them?"

"They both headed up toward the greenhouse after the flip," I said.

"Both boys?"

"Yes. They cut through the woods."

"Did they say anything?"

"No."

I had just been to Bible School and Mr. Barnes had said that God looks down and sees everything. God knew what I was up against with Clyne on the one hand and the State Trooper on the other.

"Honey, if you saw anything at all the day that Clyne flipped you, now is the time to say it. They think that Clyne may have done something to the boy who you saw him with that day."

State Trooper Rogers didn't say anything, and Aunt Adair asked me again if I had seen anything else that morning, anything at all. I had seen everything that morning. It happened two feet away from me. Clyne said if I told, I would receive a see-no-evil and he would also take Nana's eyes and my mother's eyes.

"No," I said.

My mother said, "You shouldn't have said anything to Clyne."

"Clyne had been standing by the sandbox . . ." I was going to explain then stopped talking. I felt like Davey in *Davey and Goliath* on channel five in New York. I was in a *Davey and Goliath* mess. If I had a talking dog like Goliath, he would be able to speak to Clyne and say:

Rodney didn't tell on you.

After the State Trooper left, my mother said, "You shouldn't have said anything. I do that, you see. It's because I people please. I'm a people pleaser."

8

MAGGOT'S FUNERAL HOME, THE JONES BOYS, AND PERSEUS THE PIMP

That night when Nana went to play her service at Maggot's Funeral Home, my mother sat at the kitchen table with Uncle Andy and told stories of her days growing up.

"Mother knew everybody in the coffins. When we were growing up, she never missed a funeral. We would sit right smack in the front row while mother played the organ with Tootsie sitting beside her on the bench. Do you remember that, A? If anyone came close to Mother, Tootsie would growl. Mother had fourteen Toy Manchesters when Daddy was alive. They all stayed inside and tinkled all over the house. Everywhere."

My mother took us all upstairs and showed us the sewing machine cover with the flowers on it.

"The Toy Manchesters tinkled all over it every single day. Mother would have to keep washing it."

The top Toy Manchesters were Tootsie and Laddy. One of the large portraits hanging in the den showed my grandfather holding them, one in each arm with Nana standing right behind him, with black hair.

"Tootsie and Laddy followed mother everywhere and growled at strangers."

All the cousins had heard the stories about Tootsie and

Laddy, how they had growled if anyone came close to Nana.

"The other twelve tinkled anywhere they wanted, but Tootsie and Laddy were the two that mother brought with her to the Funeral Home. Funerals damaged me for life. I'm damaged, damaged for life. We'd all be sitting there, and the families would come in crying. Dear God, every funeral, we'd all be sitting in there. Mother would say, 'That was a cold one, Rindy Anne. Elsie Goins didn't cry once. Did you notice that, Rindy Anne? I thought Molly cried the most, didn't you, Rindy Anne?'

Florence Grommet and I snuck into Maggots and hid in their caskets. We would try them all out.

'I love this one the best,' Florence would say. She had a big crush on the funeral director.

Mother hated me going around with Florence Grommet, but I did it anyway, no matter what she said. Mother used to beat me because she thought Florence was below my stature. That's why I climbed out my window every chance I got to meet Florence. We'd try out every new casket. During the summer, we'd lay in them to cool off. On the really hot days, Florence and I would go out to the lake to be baptized. Most of the time we just sat in front of Maggot's with the rest of them.

'Oh she looks so bad, I think she has cancer.'

It was always cancer, 'she looks like she has cancer.' They'd all sit out there and talk about everybody who came to the service."

The next morning after Cream of Wheat, Duncan and I

jumped off the front porch and ran into the front yard.

"Cancer, it looks like she has cancer. You remember your mom telling us how they all said that?"

"It looks like she has cancer," I said.

"Looks like she has cancer, looks like she has CANCER!" Duncan yelled. We yelled it again and again, and both of us couldn't stop laughing.

~

The State Trooper parked his car in the driveway, and for the next two days, I stood behind the curtain of Nana's upstairs window and watched him pick through the woods on the sandbox side of the house. Never once did he walk over to the Florist Shop Road or into the garden.

Even though the Trooper had a gun, I went outside only with the cousins and before I did, always examined the driveway from the window at the top of the stairs. If we walked along the Florist Shop Road, I never once turned my head in the direction of the garden or my eyes would have shot like an arrow straight toward the tadpole pond. I didn't want to look at the tadpole pond. The swelling in the woods became louder than usual at night. I lay in bed listening to its come and go, just like I had laid on the beach in Asbury Park with the waves washing over me, one after another, over and over.

That week, Uncle Ted visited, and the adults told stories

about the coal mining days. I wrote down as many of their stories as I could remember on my yellow pad then hid it in my suitcase with my baseball cards.

My granddaddy spent seventy years in the coal mines then bought a mine using the money he had saved. He had saved every single penny! You must all know this. The miners respected both my granddaddy and my daddy, you see, but not the others because they came off as too grand.

I had to grow up with that. After granddaddy bought the coal mine, the miners' children would spit on me. The miners didn't like the coal operators, you see. Hated us. Everything changed after he bought the mine. They thought we were too grand, you see. That's the way they all thought back then, but they were wrong. We weren't grand at all. Uncle William thought he was grand and moved to Knoxville. He thought he was above us all. My daddy stayed right here and was up in the mines every morning at four o'clock.

To this day, I remember an old holy roller following me all the way home from school. 'Did you read your Bible?' she kept asking. 'Did you read it? Did you?' Cursing me all the way and I mean cursing. I was walking up the driveway crying, and I just remember her following me then standing there yelling that I would be cursed to hell on earth and that my sons and daughters would be cursed as well. Mm mm. For years, I thought that was it. I believed that we were all cursed to hell on earth. I finally told Daddy, and all he did was laugh. That's why I loved my Daddy. He just laughed.

All the cousins had heard the story of how Uncle Ted had been buried alive. I always listened as carefully as I could when one of the adults told it.

All the miners carried guns back then and would shoot you at the drop of a hat. We were always afraid of being kidnapped after grandpa bought the coal mine. They would put bricks in women's pantyhose and try to kill the coal operators. Those were the days of John L. Lewis. They would ride in bulletproof cars and blow their horns, the organizers. It was right to organize but not the way they did it. And burying Uncle Ted alive like that? Mmm mm.

'Bloody Harlan' they called it.

The Jones Boys buried Uncle Ted standing straight up in the ground, buried him alive. They stuck Uncle Ted in the ground like a fence post and covered him right up to the top of his head. If it weren't for that one miner who circled back through the woods and cleared some space around Uncle Ted's nose, he would have smothered to death.

His head was sticking straight out of the ground with dirt up to his eyes, buried alive!

District 19, where we are, is the most violent in the country.

Nana said there was a man named Albert Pass who was treasurer for UMW District 19.

They called him Little Hitler.

Little Hitler organized the Jones Boys. The Jones Boys were miners who terrorized coal operators.

Lawsie Mercy, there must have been a hundred of them. They dynamited tipples and forced the drivers to shovel loads off their trucks.

When Uncle Ted arrived, Nana opened the living room and let him sit on the living room couch. I had never seen either a man or woman sit on Nana's living room couch.

Ted, can you tell us all what happened? Aunt Adair asked. She had already told the cousins that she was planning on goading Uncle Ted on to tell his story.

Yes, I can, Uncle Ted said. *We had daily apprehension for the Jones boys. That didn't prevent us from joking, but the threat of the Jones boys was unusually strong that week. Irving Johnson, our yard man, showed me his raincoat, and I passed our pony driver, and the lead pony jumped forward when the men caught me and dragged me to a shallow drain. They placed me face down in a water hole at first.*

'Go in the mines and bring the rest of the miners out,' he told them. Then he told me about not signing the UMWA contract.

While I was lying there, I saw them all crossing the ditch. I was trying to remember as many of them as I could.

'How would you like your family to see you as you are now?' one of them said.

Each one was instructed to strike me in the head with his fist. If the blow wasn't hard enough, they were told to do it again. They had already dug a hole, and they put me into it straight up then filled it in. I felt the weight of the dirt with each shovel full.

'Cover his goddamn face. Do you want to pray for this son of a bitch preacher?'

'Hell no!' they answered.

There are two sides to every story. But that wasn't right what they did on that day.

"Hell No!" Duncan yelled as soon as we got outside into the driveway. Shaw picked up a hand full of gravel and scattered it down into the garden. After that, all of us started throwing gravel at the Florist Shop sign.

"Hell no," I said before each throw. It was easier to hit the sign when I shouted *hell no!*

That night, after Uncle Ted left, all of us sat in the den. I was on the side of the couch with no carpeting and pushed my foot down into the thick layer of polyurethane while my mother started talking about Grandma Matthews.

Talk about mean; Grandma Matthews was mean as a snake. She could wring two chickens by the neck at the same time. I was talking to grandma, and she grabbed two chickens by the neck and started twirling them around while she was talking to me, just picked them up and swung them. Oh, grandma, I used to say. She was just a little thing but tough, dear GOD. She'd drown kittens. She'd put baby kittens in a burlap sack, pulled the car over and tossed them over the bridge. Or she just put them in a sack and drown them in the lake herself. Didn't like strays. Uh huh. Couldn't stand any strays.

Toward the end, she got out of hand, though. She'd wake me up and ask, 'Who are you?'

'Rindy Anne, Granma.'

'No, you're not.' She'd say.

Then I'd make something up, tell her I was Dixie and she'd say, 'No, you're not. You're Rindy Anne.' Like that, all the time. She took off her clothes and walked all the way to the bank. That was when it started to go downhill. Hung up on sex. Mmm mm. 'cover up those white legs. The boys will get you.'

When Nana went to the bathroom, my mother whispered to me,

Mother is a little like that too. She can be mean as a snake.

~

After my mother had finished talking about Grandma Matthews, Aunt Adair changed the subject: "I believe what Perseus said about Clyne. Perseus would know. He's a pimp and hears about every murder and every single robbery."

"Dear God NO, Adair! Perseus a PIMP?"

I had heard my mother tell Dad that Perseus was a pimp. My mother was acting surprised. She was people pleasing again.

People pleasing is hell. I can't stop. It's hell.

"Rindy, didn't you know that Perseus was a pimp?" Aunt Adair said.

"Dear God NO! A PIMP!?" my mother said.

I can't help it. It's called people pleasing, and I'm a people pleaser. I'll say something just to please somebody else. I hate it, but I can't help it. I hope you're never a people pleaser. It's living a life of hell.

I felt sorry for my mother because I could see whenever she started people pleasing, she couldn't stop and living in hell on earth. My mother usually started laughing before a joke had finished to please the person telling the joke. She didn't know when the punch line was coming and didn't care. I stayed still when she did that because the person might stop telling the joke and start to look around at the other people while my mother kept laughing her head off. She lived in people pleasing hell.

"Perseus is a pimp, and everybody in town knows Perseus is a pimp. He's up there right this minute selling dope at mother's florist shop!"

Nana said, "Perseus is not a pimp, Adair."

"Perseus is an alcoholic," my mother said.

"He doesn't look like a pimp, Dinah, but he is," Aunt Adair said. "Can you imagine that? What woman would be Perseus's whore?"

"Adair." Nana spoke in her deep voice and nodded toward the cousins on the couch. I wished more than anything in the world that while I sat in the den, I could keep my yellow pad on my lap and write down everything being said as it was all of great interest. I wanted more than anything in the world to do nothing else but write down every single word of what other people said.

"Dear GOD, Adair, you're right, what woman would," my mother said.

Uncle Andy said, "Mother, they're all saying the Matthews Florist Shop is the biggest whorehouse in town. I heard a teller at the bank say it this morning. She said Perseus is up there at Dinah D. Matthews whore house making wreaths."

My mother said, "No, she didn't say that, did she A? Dear God."

Nana puffed her bottom lip out.

"Of course, she didn't say that," Aunt Adair said. "Andy."

"Big Perseus," Uncle Andy said.

When Uncle Andy said *Big Perseus*, you imagined that Perseus was the President of the United States. When Uncle Andy saw the cousins, and said, *here come the communists*, it sounded as if we were the communists.

"Perseus drinks. You can smell it." my mother said. "He's up there drinking right now. I think he keeps it in the refrigerator behind the fresh cut flowers."

When we were up in New York, my mother always said: *Dad drinks. I can smell it under his door.*

She yelled at Dad through his study door when he was in the apartment. Dad never once opened up when she did that.

He's in there drinking right this minute. I can smell it. Dad, I can smell it!

I didn't care what Dad did and wished he would come down to Tennessee. My mother told me that her Daddy, whom she had loved more than anybody in the world, drank whiskey and had kept a bottle in his back pocket wherever he went.

Mother would be down there at night smashing Daddy's whiskey bottles against the basement wall.

"Perseus drinks more and more every day. Munro said Perseus's girlfriend told him, 'If he keeps this up, I'm going to charge him like everybody else.'"

"Adair, MM mm." My mother had to pinch her nose to keep from laughing. "MM mm. Mother works Perseus practically to death, poor old thing. He just needs the money."

"That's just some ole story that people like to tell that isn't true," Nana said. "I already asked Perseus if he was a pimp and Perseus told me, 'Mrs. Matthews, I am sure as hell NOT a pimp. Who would tell you that I was a pimp?'"

"Mother, of course, he's going to say that," Adair said. "He works at the Top Hat. Munro has seen him there with his prostitute."

After the adults had finished talking about Perseus, the den became quiet. After a full minute, Nana said, "Well. I'll say."

After another full minute, Uncle Gavin said, "I'll tell you."

I liked to practice saying *well,* or *I'll tell you* when I was by myself either walking through the garden or laying on my bed looking at the ceiling.

After Uncle Gavin said his last "I'll tell you," Nana said,

"Oh Gavin, I'm going to need my B12!" She patted both hands on tops of her knees. Uncle Gavin was a doctor and my mother called him *Old Gavin* even though he was younger than her.

Old Gavin looks so tired. Always tired. Just look at him sitting there. GOD, I wish he would get some rest but he won't. He never stops. He was always the helper, always helping, poor Gavin. Mother used to work him to death.

Uncle Gavin kept his black doctor's bag in the trunk of his LTD. The sound of the LTD's trunk closing out in the driveway meant someone was going to get a shot. When he brought the black bag into the den, the next thing you heard was it unsnapping.

B12s were the most popular shot in the family. Uncle Gavin kept three vials of B12 in his doctor's bag for reunions. The adults liked B12s and would say to each other:

Sounds like you need your B12.

They asked Uncle Gavin: *Gavin, could you give me a B12?*

When a cousin got a shot, Uncle Gavin told us: *This is going to be a little bee sting.* Then, after the shot, when he was breaking off the needle, he'd say, *Now I know that hurt.*

Uncle Gavin gave each cousin the empty syringe after their B12. We took them out in the driveway and shot water into each other's faces and couldn't stop laughing.

9

HAIRS, A BIGGER DARE, AND OLD MAY'S REVENGE

Before going to bed that night, Duncan came into my room, jumped up into the air, landed hard on the bed, pulled one side of his pants down and yelled:

"Hairs, Roddoh!"

Duncan had hairs!

"Hairs, Roddoh, Hairs!" he shouted. Hairs meant everything to Duncan, and I was happy for him. I also wanted hairs more than anything in the world.

After his important announcement, Duncan left, and in a few minutes I heard the hallway floorboards creak then Nana say, "Mercy."

The springs of the old armchair by my mother's door squeaked and I knew Nana had just lowered herself backward and was about to let herself drop. Every single time she dropped back, the chair's springs squeaked right before it scooted back and banged against the wall.

"Mother, Dear God in heaven, I had no idea Perseus was a pimp until Adair told me. Apparently, everybody in town knows it. And him up there working up at the Florist Shop with you in the house by yourself."

"Perseus is not a pimp, Rindy Anne," Nana said. "No one

thinks that."

I stopped listening, turned over in bed and looked out my window at the streetlight across the driveway. Moths flew against the glass, over and over. Lightning bugs twinkled between the trees as the woods rose and fell:

Dt dhh   dhdh

Dt dhh   dh

Dt dhh   dh dh

I got out of bed and turned the window crank. With the window open, the woods in Tennessee were louder than crashing waves at Asbury Park.

DT DHH   DH DH

DT DHH   DH DH

I woke up listening to the woods rise and fall as well as hearing another sound: *Gravel crunching.* I knew that meant a car was slowly creeping up the Florist Shop Road. My clock said three and it was still pitch black except for the streetlamp's glow across the drive. I sat up in bed as soon as the crunching stopped. I heard a door creak open then squeak once. Only Munro's truck door squeaked once. I didn't hear the truck door close, so I climbed out of bed and pressed my head against the screen but couldn't see past the driveway. The truck had parked on the other side of the house. I kept standing by the window, listening but didn't hear anything after that. The truck door had squeaked just once but the whole woods kept rising and falling and didn't stop.

~

The next morning, Shaw gave the good cousins a big dare: to wait for Old May at the end of the driveway. We had all waited for Old May before. What made this one bigger was the fact that Old May had jumped out at Shaw two weeks earlier.

She came out from around one of the pillars and tried to stab Shaw to death with a broken beer bottle.

When Aunt Adair told us the story, she looked straight at me because she knew how much I liked shooting peas. One after another, all the adults said something, either about Old May or pea shooting.

She'd like to kill you even if you were to shoot a single pea at her.

If she catches you shooting peas at her, she will slit your throat, go home and sleep like a log.

My mother waited until they'd finished before she spoke.

Her whole family is like that. They're all a product of incest.

Duncan kicked my foot. I had to hold my nose.

Rindy.

Nana nodded towards us all sitting on the couch.

Mother. She drinks. You can smell it when she comes up the driveway.

I went out in the front yard that morning with my Grumman Hellcat, a model I had glued the night before. Munro walked up to me and said,

"You'd better leave that woman alone, you know that, don't you?"

I knew then Nana had told Munro about our dare. She always shared the trouble the cousins found themselves in and Munro always said something to scare us. He also told Nana what we were doing but not every single time. If we got switched because of what he told her, he'd say we deserved it.

The punishments you receive here on earth serve to keep you from suffering an eternity of hell.

After Munro told me to leave Old May alone, he started walking away then stopped. He stood still as a statue, something normally he didn't do in the middle of the driveway. I stood still as well and waited for him to say something.

"I know you understand that when you say some words out loud, they may very well come back and bite you like a snake. But if you don't say something, what you don't say may come back and not only bite but eat you alive. If you fall into a hole and don't yell for help, do you think anybody will know where you are?"

"No," I told him.

Munro looked down into the garden then looked at me. I didn't say anything else. Munro said,

"Well. Sometimes it's hard to know what to do, isn't it?"

Munro walked away after saying that. I felt sorry for Munro. We were both worrying about Clyne.

~

I went back in the house after talking to Munro. All the cousins and adults were sitting around the kitchen table and as soon as I walked through the door, Aunt Adair said,

"Oh, Rodney. They found that State Trooper's car parked up by the mines. The same State Trooper that spoke to you here in the kitchen has now gone missing. They've been looking for him for two whole days."

I remembered the State Trooper standing there holding his round hat in front of him.

"Too much," my mother said. "They don't know but think something may have happened to him. He's inexperienced, you see, and didn't know what he was dealing with or who these people are up there. They only fond his empty car. Nothing. Dear God, it's just so sad. He has a wife and young baby. We know the Rogers. I went to school with his mother Jo Ann."

I had a hard time moving after that, remembering the red-haired boy's leg, smooth as ivory, lifting out of the water then sinking back down. When Clyne pulled Red into the woods, he hadn't looked worried about anything, like he'd been dragging a heavy log. Pulling Red through the woods was just part of his day's work.

Even though Aunt Adair, Nana, and Munro all told us to leave Old May alone, after breakfast Cameron, Lillian and I went down to the end of the driveway. All we did was look up Tennessee Avenue, waiting for Old May to crest the top of the hill. We weren't going to rock her and didn't bring peashooters. Cameron and I only brought one loaded squirt gun each but not to squirt, only hold up like James Bond. We were bending around the stone pillar and didn't expect a big crash and suddenly see Old May lunging out of the woods right behind us, yelling, talking, limping, twisting and *hup hup HUP HUPPING*, holding her big butcher knife in one hand, like the star in *Bird with The Crystal Plumage*.

"Old May! Old May!" Lillian shouted.

"Old May!" Cameron shouted. "Run as fast as you can, Rodney! Run, Lilly, RUN!

We ran half way up the driveway, stopped and turned. Old May wasn't behind us.

"She went into the woods," Cameron said.

We kept running all the way to the front door, slipped inside and locked the door behind us. While I ran, I wasn't all that afraid of Old May because the whole time we were waiting for her, I had been thinking about what it might be like having my eye gouged out during a see-no-evil. My see-no-evil thoughts were like the second floor bathtub filling up with water and overflowing.

Old May came up to the back door and told Nana we'd been rocking her. I told Nana that wasn't true, that we had never rocked Old May and that I didn't know any cousins who had. I had rocked Old Perseus, but he hadn't minded.

Perseus never said one word to Nana about the cousins rocking him because he loved cursing at us as much as we loved rocking him. Now and then a cousin might climb into one of the dogwoods and throw a berry or shoot a pea at Old May, but we never rocked her. We sometimes waited up in Nana's room and shot squirt guns through the screen when she passed underneath, but she never noticed being squirted when we did.

Later on, Duncan whispered to me that Shaw had rocked her the week before and didn't tell anybody.

"He rocked her good too."

An hour later, I was sitting at the kitchen table when Munro came up to the back door and told Nana through the screen:

"Mrs. Matthews, May Vanover moved her bowels in their sandbox again. There's two of them."

I didn't budge an inch. Nana had been cleaning the refrigerator with its door open, and I was sitting on the long seat around the corner eating a Debbie Cake. She couldn't see me and had forgotten I was there.

"Munro, I want you to clean out that sandbox and haul us up some new white sand."

I went straight out front and told the cousins about the two bowel movements in the sandbox. We were more excited than we had ever been in our entire lives. I had forgotten about Clyne.

"Oh my God Roddoh, she's using the sandbox as a commode!" Duncan said.

We went back inside. My mother said she already knew about the logs of dook and had known for a long time.

"She knows EXACTLY what she's doing. She sleeps in those woods behind the sandbox. Munro finds her back there all the time doing her business."

It turned out that my mother had known that Old May left her snakes under the cousin's swing set on a regular basis and that Nana had ordered Munro to shovel Old May's dook every morning and bring in new clean white sand with his truck every afternoon.

"I've always known about it. I would find them out there. Big ones. They made me SICK. I think she gets very VERY angry, and that's how she then gets her revenge, you see. That's what I think. She does it on purpose. Oh, she does."

While I had been listening in the kitchen, Munro had told Nana: *I believe she's sending your grandchildren a message.*

"Mother MAKES Munro go out in the woods to find every one of Old May's movements. And he hates it. HATES it. I hear him out there cursing."

"Where else does she leave her movements?" I asked my mother.

"Oh I don't know," my mother said. My mother told me she didn't know, but she knew. I was extremely interested, and if Dad had been there, he would have been extremely interested as well.

Duncan told me Nana was keeping it a secret. My mother knew all the locations. She told Uncle Gavin exactly where

Old May's most recent bowel movements were; Uncle Gavin told Duncan, Duncan looked then told me. Duncan had seen the one on the picnic table bench right before Munro had cleaned it up.

"OF COURSE she knows what she's doing. Of course, she does. She knows EXACTLY what she's doing," my mother said. "Old May is doing all that on purpose, you see. She's smarter than she looks, but that eye makes her look hideous. She has beautiful facial features except for that EYE."

After that the other cousins went out to play in the front yard. I didn't because I had remembered hearing Munro's truck door creak open then squeak in the middle of the night. I needed to investigate so I slipped out the screen door and walked across the Florist Shop Road. At the top of the steps, I saw the shiny button laying in the gravel but didn't bend down because I was afraid to touch it after seeing the engraving. I kicked the button off the road's ledge into the cat grass where the black snake lived then walked down the steps. I looked down into the dirt but didn't see tracks anywhere because the ground had been raked. I hadn't been back in the garden since Duncan and I performed our investigation. The stick I had left in the middle of the tadpole pond wasn't there, and the water had risen to the very top, higher than I had ever seen it and now drizzled over the wall onto the ground. Someone had gathered all the sticks and leaves that had been laying anywhere nearby and piled them up along some other fresh cut branches right in front of the tadpole pond. A big limb of an Oak as well as an old rotten log lay across the pond now from one side to the other. I couldn't get close to the wall even if I wanted to.

I heard gravel crunch and ran back up the garden steps. Munro stepped around holly tree at the corner of the house and started walking up the Florist Shop Road then stopped when he caught sight of me. I waved. Munro raised his hand then pushed his cap farther back onto his head and began walking toward me.

"May Vanover's mad as a hornet and went and told her brother that you were the one that rocked her. I told her you weren't the one."

I told Munro: "I never rocked Old May and have shot as many peas at her as any of the other cousins have."

Munro said, "That don't matter. You're the one staying here, and you're the one she's used to seeing. Now your kin are fixing on leaving so you'll be center of her attention. Her brother's worse than she is. He'll come up here, shoot you then go home and put on a pot of coffee."

My stomach was turning when I went back inside the house. Now Clyne, Old May, and her brother were all after me. I was glad I hadn't been able to look down into the tadpole   pond.

10

FILL YOUR HANDS, SHELDON'S SHOE STORE, AND A DOG IN THE COUSIN'S TENT

That Saturday night we drove the Olds and Comet around the Loop to the Crystal, ordered cheeseburgers and milkshakes to go, then headed over to the highway drive-in and saw *True Grit*.

Rooster Cogburn said: *Fill your hands, you son of a bitch!* He put the reins between his teeth and rode across the field, firing his rifle at Tom Chaney and his gang.

My mother had been crunching popcorn when he did that and whispered: "Old John Wayne. I think he has throat cancer."

After the movie, as we were pulling out onto the highway, flames and sparks leapt far up into the sky on the big hill opposite the drive-in. A fog had closed in and the ride home was like driving the Olds through a lump of coal. The flames leaped off the burning telephone pole so bright that you couldn't see anything apart from the grass on the side of the hill, rolling out like a green carpet all the way to the highway. In New York, you would have heard sirens coming but when I asked my mother if anybody called the Fire Department, she said:

"No. Nobody here is going to call them. The Fire

Department is probably already up there."

Nana said, "Oh just hush, Rindy."

I kept my eyes glued through the back window of the Olds, following the flames until they disappeared around the bend.

Duncan said, "Fill your hands, you son of a bitch."

I said, "Fill your hands, you son of a bitch."

We passed Griffiths Department Store right before hitting the Crystal and were slowing down to turn up the Loop when we spotted the men standing at the stop light.

"Don't look. They're trying to flag us into their meeting, you see. They want to see who is in the cars."

When they started walking over to the Olds, my mother said:

"Don't look at them. Even if they call you by your name."

Duncan and I ducked down in the back seat. The men wore hoods with eye holes cut out, like scarecrows and came right up to the back window and looked in.

The next morning, we all went to church. Mr. Barnes sang the doxology. After he sang, *Praise Father son and holy ghost. Ahhh mennnn,* he waved the congregation down like closing the lid of a box. I had seen him close the lid many times and loved closing the lid myself more than any other church gesture in the world.

After closing the lid, I loved repeating the word *congregation* and singing, *Praise God for all ye blessings flow!* Even if I was by myself, I couldn't help but laugh every time I said *congregation* and usually couldn't stop.

The pipes of the church organ sat behind the pulpit at the back of the stage. When Nana brought her hands down on the organ's keys, the notes blew from the pipes as loud as the Southern Railway train horn passing in front of the crossing gate. Everyone knew that the doxology was coming.

Bible School was held in the basement, the church service upstairs. We all went to church at nine o'clock, Bible School at eleven. My mother drove back and picked me up in the church parking lot at twelve-thirty.

The summer before, I woke up one Saturday with both cheeks as big as grapefruits and had to stay at Nana's house for two Sundays in a row. I didn't have to go to either church or Bible School. I wanted more than anything in the world to contract the mumps again this summer, so I wouldn't have to go to church for two weeks; but Uncle Gavin said once you get them, you become immune.

Mr. Barnes was the minister as well as the Bible School teacher. He wore a suit as if he worked at the First National Bank. Mr. Barnes talked more about John the Baptist than he talked about Moses and more about Jesus than John the Baptist, but not much more. Mr. Barnes talked about the Ishmaelites, the Pharisees, and the Sadducees, and always went through the *Beholds*, the *blessed are thoses*, the *blessed are yous*, the *before the cock crows twices*, as well as the *I am going fishings*.

Mr. Barnes knew a lot about John the Baptist. I don't

know how he knew as much as he did but he told us that John the Baptist wore a leather belt, a camel hair shirt and ate katydids. John Bass said John the Baptist ate crawdads. The Basses went to the Methodist Church. The Methodist John the Baptist ate crawdads, the Baptist one katydids.

Oh, it's a good church, very good. Less guilt, far less guilt. And why not. Why NOT! I wanted to join the Methodist church when I was young and mother forbid it. There was an evangelist there who wanted me to join. Oh, he was always just so nice to me and was always saying just how much he liked me. He may have even had a thing about me; I don't know. But the bank president went there, doctors, lawyers. Some people are suspicious of that, you see. When I was growing up, they would whisper, 'He's a Methodist, a Methodist, whisper whisper.' The coal operators went to the Methodist church, you see, and everybody thought they were so grand.

Mr. Barnes said John the Baptist didn't care what other people thought. I told my mother Mr. Barnes said that and she said:

The thing about it was John the Baptist was NOT a people pleaser. He was just the opposite, maybe too much the other way. They say he smelled.

Mr. Barnes said John the Baptist knew Jesus was the son of God and had been hard on Jesus because of that. He knew Jesus couldn't make excuses for himself but also knew that being the son of God was a tough position to be in. Mr. Barnes told us John the Baptist stayed down by the banks of the river Jordan, got dust all over his face and all over his clothes. I didn't know how Mr. Barnes knew all these details, so I asked him

How do you know John the Baptist was mean to Jesus?

Not mean, stern.

I imagined John the Baptist sternly saying: *Fill your hands, you son of a bitch!*

Mr. Barnes didn't say John the Baptist swore, but I think John the Baptist did swear, like Perseus or Rooster Cogburn. John the Baptist wasn't related to God and wasn't a people pleaser. I couldn't stop imagining John the Baptist covered in dust, standing out in the hot sun on the banks of the river saying, *Fill your hands, you son of a bitch.*

I liked saying *John the Baptist* out loud just as much as I liked saying *son of a bitch.*

I imagined if Duncan said *John the Baptist* out loud then went on to repeat that name over and over and over until the name didn't make sense, we would probably start laughing and wouldn't stop.

Mr. Barnes told us the woman Salome had said: *Give me the head of John the Baptist on a platter.*

Nana used a platter for meat loaf and sometimes watermelon. I felt sorry for John the Baptist and asked Mr. Barnes if there were real tortures in hell. He asked me why was it that I didn't know there were real tortures. He said he would tell me why but went on to explain the reason I didn't know was that I was from New York and people in New York didn't know all they should about hell. I told Mr. Barnes that my mother said *Hell is on this earth.* Mr. Barnes looked down at his papers in front of him and didn't say anything for a while.

In New York, my mother brought old ladies over to our apartment. The ladies cured themselves with prayer. It was one of those old ladies who told my mother that hell was on this earth and after she told her that, my mother always said that the lady was *absolutely right*, that *hell was on this earth*.

Dad told me: *Your mother can't stop helping these women. It's remarkable. She has to help these women. Has to.*

My mother said: *Janey told me the old women represent my mother and I'm trying to help them because I'm trying to help Mother. That's what Janey told me, and I think she's ABSOLUTELY RIGHT.*

My mother always said *right* in a loud voice and told me things that her friend Janey said and what Janey thought.

Why else would I be doing it? I can't stop pleasing them, and I hate it. I have to please them. I hate every minute of pleasing them.

One day, my mother had told me that she was bringing over an old lady who had been blind then, after she prayed, got her eyesight back.

She's big in the church, very big, my mother told me. My mother picked the old woman up and brought her to our apartment. I purposefully stayed in my room when they came through the door, but my mother came in and said, *Rodney, there's someone here who wants to meet you.* I already knew it was the big one from church who had been blind. I had started worrying about meeting her before she got to the apartment because I knew she was going to test my faith. When I came out into the living room to meet the old woman, before she said a hello or a nice to meet you, she asked:

Do you believe in God, Rodney?

This was the one question I did not want her to ask. The woman looked me straight in the eye, and I didn't know what to say. I wasn't sure if I had the right answer. Dad thought God was all shit, but I didn't know what I thought. My mother stood next to the woman and said,

Go ahead and answer. It's ok.

The lady didn't take her eyes off me for a second. She knew all about God and was so big in church that she might have already read my mind. God might have already told her that I wasn't sure. Both the lady and my mother stood still, waiting for me to answer. I had to people please right then and there so I said:

Yes.

The old lady didn't say anything. I wasn't sure if the answer pleased her or if she knew I was lying my head off. I was glad to get back to my room and didn't make any noise after that, just sat on my bed and waited until she left.

After a while, Mr. Barnes shuffled his papers and said, *Well* then spoke very slowly to me as if I was from France and this was my first day in Bible School. Very slowly he explained that there was an eternal hell run by the devil and that for some people, hell was on this earth, and that hell on earth might be true but that nothing on the face of the earth could ever match the hell of hell.

I raised my hand again and told Mr. Barnes that my father said there were some thoughts and memories that a man couldn't bear to think. I told him Dad said a person's body would pretend the memory never happened and that a man didn't have any control over that kind of pretending if

111

the body didn't want to remember something. I told him Dad said a person would be living in hell because he would find himself caught between two worlds.

"There is no punishment on earth that is as bad as eternal damnation," Mr. Barnes answered right away and didn't want anybody to ask any more questions after that.

When I got back to Nana's, Shaw explained what they didn't tell you in the Bible: *Jesus was tortured.*

Uncle Andy said that the real Jesus was tortured by Roman soldiers.

"He was nailed to a cross by soldiers and speared. The soldiers just laughed. They didn't care who he was. They nailed one person after another to the crosses. "

Uncle Andy knew what soldiers did. They nailed Jesus to a big cross then hoisted up in the air. The soldiers held one of his feet on top of the other then drove nails through both. They drove nails through his hands as well, right into the wood. It could have been a door or the side of a barn but a wooden cross was easier to stick into the ground.

"That's torture. The soldiers in the Roman Army tortured the shit out of him before he died. Some people think he's not the son of God, that he's just some man that talked too much and ended up getting tortured."

Shaw had grown up in Alaska, Korea and Turkey, all the places where Uncle Andy had been stationed. Shaw knew all about torture and had explained to me how the Japanese had cut the balls off American soldiers during World War II and squeezed them from five feet away. The American soldiers could feel their balls being squeezed by *radar* and the Japanese knew that. Shaw also told me that the first thing Turks did when they got an American into prison was knock out all his teeth with a sledge hammer.

"That's the very first thing they do, Roddoh," Shaw said. After Shaw told me that, I couldn't stop thinking about the Turks knocking the American's teeth out the very first thing. I wondered whether to ask Mr. Barnes about Jesus getting tortured during the next Bible School class but decided I wouldn't.

~

Nana had ordered a big canvas tent from Couch's Hardware for us to play in and that afternoon, Munro began setting it up in the front yard. I watched him from my upstairs window and saw something unusual sticking out behind the big Oak where he usually hid to smoke his Winstons: A knee. Uncle Andy had already said that Munro might be trying to hide Clyne from the Sheriff's department and for us to be careful if we went outside.

He might very well be out there still. I wouldn't go out by yourselves until they lock him up.

All the cousins were up at the Florist Shop rocking Old Perseus, and because I thought there was a chance the knee might belong to Clyne, I went downstairs and asked Nana if I could to town with her to get my shoes.

Nana clapped her hands together and in a loud voice, said: "OH HONEY!"

Every single summer, Nana took me down to Sheldon's to buy shoes. I only wore them for church, and they hurt.

"Let me go ahead and make a call, right quick," Nana said. Nana always called ahead and asked to speak directly to Mr. Sheldon himself.

"Well, how you Sam, so good to hear your voice. Now I'll be bringing down my grandson Rodney, who came all the way from New York for his shoes."

Mr. Sheldon was always behind the counter at his store waiting with his horn to slip on the new pair of shoes. A girl measured my size on the machine then Mr. Sheldon came out with the box under one arm, took the shoes out and cradled them like a baby for me to see.

"My, what pretty shoes," Nana said.

I didn't like getting shoes and only said I wanted to go because I didn't want to be at the house that afternoon. I didn't know if the knee behind the tree belonged to Clyne but couldn't think who else the knee would have belonged to. I examined the front yard very carefully when Nana and I were climbing into the Olds and kept turning my head as we pulled down the drive but still couldn't see who was behind the Oak. Whoever it was had moved as the Olds moved. Someone knew I was watching.

We took the Loop all the way around town, made a left turn at the drive-in and headed out the highway toward Griffith's to pick up a gallon of milk first. When we passed the big hill that had been lit up by flames the night before, the telephone pole had been taken down. The hill was dull and empty, its wide green lawn stretching all the way down to the highway without a single scorch mark. The big white house sitting at the top was called *The Mansion.* No one lived there. Nana said that every spring someone gave The Mansion a new coat of white paint.

I suppose so it could look respectable. It's been there almost since the Civil War days and is about fixing to fall.

Sheldon's Shoe Store sat right beside the Five-and-Dime. Nana said Sheldon's was a better shoe store than most of them in Knoxville.

Sheldon's is known far and wide.

Sheldon's was always open on Sunday after church because Mr. Sheldon was Jewish.

The Sheldons are the only Jews in the whole county we know about.

Nana was friends with Mr. Sheldon and he had told her the story of the Sheldon Family. They had come into town a hundred years ago, over the mountains, pulling a wagon. The Sheldons opened up a knife sharpening shop at first. Mr. Sheldon's mother knew there weren't any Jews in the county for little Mr. Sheldon to play with and knew there wasn't going to be a synagogue where little Mr. Sheldon could go so she sent him to military school in Chattanooga.

She knew, my mother said. *Mrs. Sheldon was the matriarch.*

My friends Barry Gross, Bubbles Berger, Ellen Katz and Nick Feigenbaum all said they were Jewish, and I had been over to every one of their houses. The Cohens lived in the apartment right below ours. My mother said the Cohens were Jewish but never went to their synagogue. Mr. Cohen was like Dad. He didn't care, but Andrea and Edmund got

Hanukah presents. They had a terrace right below our kitchen window. Mr. Cohen had to sleep in the living room because someone tried to break in through their terrace door every single night of the week. Mr. Cohen woke up and threw a shoe at the door then went back to sleep. My mother said he didn't care, he just slept in the living room and threw a shoe at the door whenever he heard it rattle. I played with Edmund and Andrea Cohen every week and wanted to marry Andrea, but Andrea reached puberty and got hairs. Edmund had his own yarmulke and threw it like a Frisbee when he came up to my living room.

I went with Bubbles Berger when he had to be dropped off and picked up from Hebrew school. I went to his brother's Bar Mitzvah and another time to synagogue when Bubbles gave me one of his yarmulkes, and I touched the scrolls. Bubbles could play anything on the drums. He wore headphones when he played. I played trombone and hated it. The music teacher needed a trombone for his band so gave me the trombone instead of the violin that I had wanted to play. My trombone teacher said: *You're a French horn, not a trombone.* I always wished I could play drums like Bubbles.

Ellen Katz had a cleft in the middle of her boobs and hairs and invited me over to her apartment. I knew she had hairs and was very curious about them so I asked and she showed me the top of them. Ellen Katz smelled like something; I'm not sure what. We kissed in her room, and I smelled her for a week afterward whenever I breathed through my nose. Her smell stayed in my nose hairs. When I touched her belt, pulling it down a little more to see her hairs, she gripped my wrist and wouldn't let go. But she didn't have to grip my wrist. I didn't have hairs and just wanted to see.

Nana said Mr. Sheldon found a Jewish woman in Chattanooga, married her and brought her back home. Mr. Sheldon was happy after that and now owned the best shoe store in the county.

Everybody in the county knows Sheldon's Shoes.

~

The next morning Shaw told the cousins that the big canvas tent Munro put up was Army Headquarters and that Uncle Andy and Aunt Adair had bought us all M16s at the Five-and-Dime. The M16s made a *rat a tat tat rata tat tat* sound when you pulled the trigger and was the most exciting present I had ever received in my life. After breakfast, we took the M16s into the front yard, cradling them in our arms like combat GIs cradled their real McCoy M16s.

Aunt Adair put a pitcher of red Kool-Aid with Dixie cups on a small card table inside the tent flap. The cousins lay our M16s against the outside wall and marched inside single file to hold our military meeting. Inside, the tent was hot and brown, like walking into the middle of a paper bag that had been set on an oven shelf. I checked my Dixie cup after each sip to see how much Kool-Aid was left and only remembered Clyne after my second or third sip. I had almost forgotten about him with my new M16.

The next day it rained hard, and the tent leaked in one of the corners. The sun came out, and by the time the Daredevil's Club held its next military meeting, the tent smelled like Nana's clothes dryer. We voted to play flashlight tag, and while we were picking the teams, Shaw heard something and stuck his head out the flap. He kept his head outside for a full minute before pulling it back in.

"There's some old dog sitting out there looking at our tent."

We took turns going over to the tent flap and examining the old gray dog. As soon as I opened the flap, the dog lowered his head, staring at me, his two eyes red as strawberries. He rose to his feet and walked right into the tent. One of his ears flopped over, and the only hair he had left was a patch growing off the side of his neck like a little tree with three bare branches. The cousins backed away and watched him wobble over to the far wall then fall. As soon as he fell, he stood back up and walked out the flap as if he had forgotten something. Shaw went over to the door again, stuck his head out, brought it back in and said the dog wasn't anywhere to be seen.

We took out M16s, ran back to the house and played in the upstairs hallway for the rest of the afternoon then came back outside after dinner for flashlight tag and squirt guns.

The next morning, the cousins were sitting at the kitchen table holding our M16s and had just decided to make the tent a Viet Nam combat base when Cameron came running through the back door and said,

"The dog's inside."

Shaw made it into a dare to go back in. Uncle Andy had told him something might be wrong with the dog and that we shouldn't get close to it, so Shaw said the dare was to touch the wall of the tent closest to the dog.

When we filed in, the dog was laying in the same spot he had sat down on the day before, but this time, he was panting hard and not moving a muscle. He growled with his mouth closed if any cousin took even one step toward him. The tent smelled like the dog and we saw his pile of doo and puddle of pee in the corner. None of us felt like playing in the tent, so we left. The next day we hoped the dog had gone, but it was still sitting in the same spot with a new puddle on the cousins' side. When we all filed in, the dog growled at us like he owned the tent.

We told Nana about the dog while she was making our griddle cakes. Nana finished what she was doing, set out the Kayo syrup, put the big platter of buttered griddle cakes in the middle of the red checked table cloth and called out the screen door to Munro. She went out back to talk to him. Shaw slid over by the screen to listen then came back to the table and said Nana had told Munro to fetch his rifle and shoot the dog. In the den that night, the cousins were told that Munro was coming early in the morning and that if any of us wanted to see him shoot the dog, we had better get up early.

While I lay in bed watching the bugs bounce off the street lamp, thinking about the wobbling dog and the three stalks of hair on his neck. I woke up with frost still on the window and listened. The mist hid the sun, and when I came downstairs, the cousins were all waiting in the kitchen. Cameron said the dog was already dead, that Munro had come before any of us had woken up, shot him, put him in his truck and drove him to the dump.

Duncan was imitating Nana. "Munro. Get your gun and shoot that dog. Shoot that dog, Munro. Munro. Unstop my commode. Munro. Come up here right quick and plunge my commode! Munro Munro Munro!"

I remembered the dog, sitting in the corner of the tent, panting.

11
SPECIAL REPORTS, THE MOLE AND THE SNAKE

The cousins didn't play in the tent after that. Most of the time I sat in Nana's room and watched TV. I didn't want to go outside because they still hadn't caught Clyne so I switched around and around the channels.

I watched wrestling because that was all that was on in Tennessee. John Bass called it *wrastlin* and the Bass cousins knew the names of all the wrastlers. Mark Bass had even been to wrastlin in Knoxville. I wasn't sure what to think about wrastlin or why people would watch it and not only watch it but shout out and jump up and down, whether they believed wrastlin was true or not. When wrastlers hit each other, their heads vibrated up and down like Daffy Duck getting walloped with a frying pan. I examined the wrastlers as carefully as I could, trying to catch them pretending. I couldn't and had to run out of the room when they started hitting each other with chairs or fell out of the ring. The wrastlers spent a lot of time chasing each other around the audience, tipping over chairs and spilling people's drinks. Everything they did was against the rules. Every now and then a wrastler got blood on his face and went down on his knees in the middle of the ring. The other wrastler would take advantage and jump off the top of the ropes coming down on the back of his head with their elbow. This was against the rules. Every single time the referee looked like he hadn't seen it happen, or had been arguing with someone else, or looking at his watch, or at the woman parading around the ring in her bathing suit holding up the number.

I would land on the Grand Ole Opry a lot while I was switching around but only stayed if I heard Minnie Pearl call out *Howwwdeeee*. I liked watching the price tag on her hat jiggle and switched as soon as she was done. They showed the cartoon *Gigantor* in Tennessee, but I was sick and tired of *Gigantor* from seeing it too many times up in New York. I liked *The Time Tunnel* and *The Green Hornet* although *The Green Hornet* was very rare in Tennessee.

When a Special Report came on, they came on quick, and if I were the only one watching, I'd yell out at the top of my lungs:

Special Report! There's a Special Report on!

My mother would yell: *Oh my God!*

We all filed into Nana's room for every Special Report. If I could, I'd sit in her rocking chair in front of the TV but had to be careful. When I pushed my foot up and down against the floor, the whole thing sometimes tipped over backward, and I'd hit my head against the bedpost. The chair tipped over so fast that I couldn't stop it but recognized what was happening, like being swallowed up in a nightmare. Before I knew it, I was tipping over, a second later holding the back of my head. I knew the spot would hurt for a full minute and that full minute would be a bad one, just as I knew how long my leg would hurt after getting switched and whether it helped more to yell at the top of my lungs or just squeeze my leg tight depended on which part was getting hit.

Half the time, a Special Report meant somebody had been assassinated. You never knew who it had been or when the next one was going to happen, only that someone was always going to get shot and a Special Report would come on.

My very first Special Report came on while we were in the car down in Florida. My mother said what she usually did; that I couldn't remember that far back but I remembered everything about it and every word that had been spoken by the announcer on that day. There hadn't been a Special Report like that one since. I had been driving with my mother in the Comet when the announcer came on and said:

We interrupt this program to bring you a special bulletin from ABC Radio. Here is a special bulletin from Dallas Texas. Three shots were fired at President Kennedy's motorcade today in downtown Dallas Texas.

My mother pulled the Comet over to the side of the road. We sat and listened. Other cars had already pulled over. There were three beeps then the announcer said:

There was a possibility that the President, Mister John F. Kennedy, has been seriously wounded.

Afterward, the announcer said that President Kennedy had been shot and that Mrs. Kennedy had grabbed her husband and cried out *Oh No.*

A woman came running out of the bank right in front of the Comet after the announcer said that. She ran into the street and stood with her hand over her face. A truck blew its horn at her because she wasn't moving out of the way.

You never knew what the announcer was going to say right after he said,

We interrupt regular programming to give you this special report.

It took a few minutes from the time the sign came up on the TV screen until the newscaster began speaking. Sometimes the special report was boring, and I switched the channel, but most of the time it was a bad surprise and everybody watching held their hands over their mouths.

The very first Special Report the came on this summer was a short one. I had been watching *Hee Haw*. The fat man in overalls had been talking very slow while the announcer who broke in was talking very fast.

We interrupt this regularly scheduled program for a Special Report.

"Special Report!" I had called out.

Glinda, the Good Witch of the North from the Wizard of Oz, had died. My mother said, "Mm mm. that's a tugger. You used to have a big crush on her." My mother didn't say anything else and walked out of the room. Last year, Dorothy had died and her Special Report lasted longer. My mother had watched the whole thing and even called Dad afterwards.

It's just so sad with everything she had to go through. She was on dope.

After Glinda's Special Report ended, the announcer said: *We now return you to your regularly scheduled program.* Nana came in, laid down on her bed and said:

"Rodney, I don't think I've ever told you the story of the

old Woodchopper."

Nana had told me the story of the old Woodchopper three or four times but had never finished telling it to me because she had always fallen asleep before the end.

I pushed my foot into the floor to make the rocking chair move, went up on tiptoes and came back down, listening.

"There once was an old Woodchopper who lived deep in the forest. He had a wife and two children whom he loved more than anything in the world. He worked from the time the sun came up to the time it set. He chopped trees all day long in the forest and once a year took the long trip into town to sell his wood. The Woodchopper had two prized possessions; one was his crosscut saw, the other, his ax. The Woodchopper owned a beautiful red ax that was made especially for him and had been a present from his wife when they were first married. The Woodchopper cherished his red ax more than any other earthly possession.

At the end of each summer, the Woodchopper loaded all the wood he had chopped on his wagon and took it into town to sell. Every single log had to be split before he loaded it. The wood paid for his family's food for the entire winter and paid for their warm clothing. That year the Woodchopper's family had been running low on food because the year before hadn't been a good one."

"What does that mean?"

"Well, the store didn't pay the old Woodchopper what they had paid him the year before for his wood so he couldn't buy as much food as he usually did to feed his family over the winter. What happened that year was that the Woodchopper and his family started running out of food even before Christmas. The poor old Woodchopper was a good man, but fell on hard times."

Nana then said that it got so bad the Woodchopper's wife had to cook the leather on the Woodchopper's shoes for their children to eat.

"The Woodchopper knew he had to go to town earlier than he usually did to sell the wood he had chopped that summer. He couldn't wait to chop more wood so he had less wood to sell and knew he would bring back less food because of that.

The Woodchopper loaded his wagon and kissed his wife and children goodbye. The Woodchopper knew it would take him many days to travel all the way to the town and back, and that he had to travel through the woods and pass over an old bridge where a mean old Troll lived. The Woodchopper usually took his trip to town later in the year when the Troll had already gone South, but this time, he had no choice. There was no other way to town through the woods but for this one road.

The Troll was a dangerous creature because you couldn't tell what he would do from one day to the next. Sometimes the Troll wouldn't even get out of bed or, if he did, wouldn't say a thing or even stand in the road but spend the day mulling around under his bridge. On other days, the Troll would be angry for no reason and wouldn't let anybody cross or would kill the person without asking them a single question. People knew to stay away from the old Troll, but in this case, the poor old Woodchopper had no choice. He had to cross the Troll's bridge to get into town and sell his wood so his family would have something to eat beside shoe leather for the long winter months."

"What was the reason the Troll would get angry?" I began to get worried about the Woodchopper.

"He was a mean Troll, and there was no way of telling what mood the Troll would be in. The Woodchopper knew that he had to be patient and polite with the Troll and ask his permission to cross the bridge. Some people weren't polite to the Troll, and the Troll would kill them.

Sure enough, the poor old Woodchopper rode along the road through the deep forest for two whole days then pulled up on one side of the bridge. It was a foggy morning, so the Woodchopper had to strain his eyes to see the road in front of him. The Troll was nowhere to be seen, and the Woodchopper thought that he might still be sleeping."

Nana stopped talking and began to snore. I let her snore for a little while then shouted, "Nana!"

She didn't wake up but only snored louder. I wanted to find out what was going to happen to the Woodchopper but went downstairs to the kitchen instead and scooped the little bit of the strawberry Neapolitan ice cream left into a bowl, the part that didn't have chocolate touching it.

~

The next morning, I opened my eyes and listened to Nana

snoring in her bed at the end of the hall. When I tiptoed past her room, she sounded like the hairless dog's snarl had in the cousin's tent. I swung around the top newel and glanced at her TV. The red, white and blue American Flag was flying across the screen. Nana's glasses sat at the very end of her nose, ready to fall off.

The dew hanging off the grass sparkled so brightly that I had to bow my head and squint toward the gravel to see where I was walking. The night before, I had heard the gravel crunch on the Florist Shop Road another time, and heard the same truck door squeak open and squeak close.

If Dad had been in Tennessee, he would have said *fascinating* and would have tried to figure out why a truck had stopped twice on the Florist shop road in the middle of the night. I had my theory as to why but didn't write it down on my yellow pad. I was careful only to write down what other people said, not my theories.

I had made up my mind after hearing the truck door squeak a second time that I would go down to the garden before anybody got up to conduct my investigation. I stood at the top of the steps and looked down into the cat grass below the spot in the road where I had kicked the little silver button with Highway Patrol stamped on it. I couldn't make out any sparkling, only green and brown.

At the bottom of the steps, I stopped. A copperhead was turned over on its side and lay in front of the gazebo. Seeing its underbelly meant it was probably already dead. Nana told Munro to kill all the copperheads he came across so the cousins wouldn't step on them. Munro used a hoe to cut their heads off and always left the body behind on the walk for us to see. Thick dark blue blood would ooze from the hole where the head had been.

This copperhead still had its head so Munro may not have been the one who had killed it. Or if he had, he was trying to scare us. I picked up a stick lying by the gazebo steps, leaned over and poked the snake then rolled it over. I made a hockey wrist shot, sending it over into the ivy against the Florist Shop Road wall then had to shove my way past the branches piled up in front of the tadpole pond to get close.

The sticks had been stacked even thicker since the last time I had been there and the rotten log had rolled off the top of the pile, making it hard to get near the wall. A streak of sun cut across the surface of the tadpole pond. I stayed still, standing on tiptoes and moving my head from side to side to get a better look at the sack. I might have been able to stretch over the branches, reach down into the water and touch it, but didn't want to. Instead, I pushed my way back out to the path and felt better the farther I moved away from the tadpole pond.

I walked down towards the Magic Fountain where the cousins usually didn't go. That part of the garden was more overgrown and every attraction had been pulled up out of the ground. The biggest attraction on that side had been a well called the Magic Fountain. No one could remember what sort of attraction it had been, only that it hadn't been a popular one. The Magic Fountain had turned into a round concrete hole. When I stepped over the weeds to have a look, I saw one of the most interesting things I had ever seen in my entire life: *a mole*.

The mole was following the inside of the Magic Fountain's wall around and around like a little blind man with two lumps for eyes and skin as white as Cream of Wheat. I could have touched the mole but didn't want to worry or scare it. The mole followed the edge of the well around, while never once moving into the middle. The cracks in the side of the wall didn't look big enough for it to have squeezed through; the fact that I didn't know where the mole had come from and that it had ended up at the bottom of the concrete hole going around and around was very mysterious.

The mole wasn't big enough to have scaled the Magic Fountain's wall.

When I went back to the house, Nana was in the kitchen fixing Cream of Wheat. I ate a big bowl full and kept thinking about the little mole and the sack I had seen in the tadpole pond. I couldn't stand it and slipped back out as soon as I finished, bringing a slice of Wonder Bread with me. When I checked the Magic Fountain, the mole was gone!

I stood still, listening for rustling or slithering and checked everywhere around the Fountain, being very careful where I stepped but couldn't find the little mole anywhere.

As there were no streaks of sun in the garden as there had been before, I pushed my way back in through the pile of sticks to get a better look at the sack under the tadpole pond's water. When Munro raked the front yard, he put the leaves into burlap bags just like the one under the water. I examined the round end for a full minute, then felt I had to sit. My own head was becoming hot as an oven so I pushed my way back out and squatted down on the ground.

Munro's truck pulled up while I was in the garden the second time and I could hear him sweeping the walkway from the house to the Florist Shop Road. When I came up the garden steps, he was holding his broom watching me. I waved. Munro didn't wave back. He started yelling and talking faster than usual.

"I would stay out of that garden if I were you. There's copperheads all around down in there."

I told Munro how I discovered the mole in the Magic Fountain and that it had mysteriously disappeared. Munro's voice rose higher and higher like an airplane taking off. He twisted his ear while he spoke.

"That mole's the devil and will lure you down there with its innocence. The boogie man walks in that garden now, and if you spend too much time down in there, he'll reach up out of the ground, grab hold of your leg and drag you to hell."

Munro went on to say the mole had already been taken down to hell by the time I got back into the house and told me again that more than likely the mole was the devil himself, disguised by innocence.

Munro knew more about hell than Mr. Barnes, my Bible School teacher did and handled snakes in church. I saw Munro's rake leaning against Nana's holly bush and wondered if it had been Clyne who raked around the tadpole pond after dropping in the bodies.

~

As well as the big black snake that lived in the cat grass on the Snow-White side of the garden, a cottonmouth curled up somewhere on top of the Press and Tribune stacked behind the basement steps. Marjorie wouldn't go down in the basement after it had shot out at her while she was carrying down the laundry basket. Nana did all the washing from that day onward.

Munro told me the basement snake was a viper and that vipers struck without warning and that's why they didn't use them for handling as much in his church. They handled mainly copperheads, every now and then a rattler. He told me that he saw the viper crawl out the basement window once and that it was so big it took five minutes to get through the hole in the glass.

I fetched my shotgun from the truck, but by the time I got back it had disappeared. The thing goes off hunting every night and sometimes comes back with a jackrabbit in its belly.

Nana always wanted me to come down to the basement to help with the laundry. I took the basement steps fast, two at a time and jumped from side to side. Nana never worried about the snake lunging out at her and took one step, rested, another step, rested, all the way down to the bottom.

It's just some old cottonmouth and won't bother you if you don't pay any attention to it.

My mother wouldn't go down to the basement if she didn't have to. She hated snakes.

I grew up with snakes everywhere and was stepping on them all the time. I hate them. HATE.

I knew most of Nana's basement but didn't know that part behind the stairs and against the back wall.

Munro said the big black snake that lived in the garden cooled off in the coal bin on the garage side of the basement. I liked the garage side of the basement better than the washing machine side. I could look straight through the furnace door at the mound of coal that had been there since my grandfather was alive with his shovel still sticking straight up at the top. I thought the garage side of the basement could be the good side. Each side had its snake. Nana didn't believe there was a good side or a bad side and said that if she could, she'd kill both snakes. Two summers before, she had found one under her bed and had called out:

Marjorie, bring us up a pot of boiling water!

When Marjorie brought the pot of boiling water up the stairs, Nana took it out of her hands and tossed it under her bed. The snake slithered out, Nana grabbed her black pistol off the night table and shot it through the head. Nobody knew Nana was going to do that. I fell back onto my bottom while my mother had to raise both arms to stop Marjorie from tipping over backward off the top step. Nana said she thought the snake had climbed up the ivy on the side of the house and slithered in through the hole in the screen to get cool under her bed.

If it doesn't belong near her, she kills it.

12
CAST IRON SAYINGS, NANA'S KNEES AND THE NIGHTMARE THAT COULDN'T BE CHANGED

After examining the burlap sack in the tadpole pond, I didn't want to leave my room for the rest of the summer. The second day after seeing the sack was worse than the first day. On the second day, the cousins had taken their M16s to play jungle combat down in the garden. I told them I was feeling sick but didn't think anyone believed me. I didn't care if they did or not. I wasn't going back down in the garden.

Instead, I spent a good deal of time standing in front of the paddles and chimes in Nana's dining room. She didn't mind a cousin standing there as long as we didn't touch anything. I liked looking at the chimes more than the paddles and could always take the mallet off its hook and hit the chimes. I could only stare at the paddles. I rang the chimes, stared at the paddles then turned and had a look at the brass cowboy ashtray sitting on the living room table, with its swinging cactus. Nothing in the living room or dining room had been moved for fifteen years since my grandfather died except for one cast iron saying hanging over the paddles. Nana had brought it in from the kitchen over the winter:

Chasten thy son while there is hope, and let not thy soul spare for his crying.

All the other cast iron sayings hung on the two walls around the red-checked kitchen table. Whenever I ate Cream of Wheat, I examined one of Nana's cast iron sayings, or I examined all of them, one after another. The first saying I came to was always *Bless This House,* which was also the shortest.

After that, I normally turned to *Yea, though I walk through the valley of the shadow of death, I shall fear no evil.* I used this cast iron saying in my nightmare if I was being chased by the Incarnation of Evil.

I paid less attention to the other sayings, although the one that took up the most room was: *Surely goodness and loving kindness will follow me all the days of my life, and I will dwell in the house of the Lord forever.* Its cast iron words were small and hard to pick out except for the word *surely.* When I blurred my eyes and looked toward that particular saying, the only word I could pick out was *surely.*

The smallest cast iron saying was: *This above all: To your own self be true.* Nana had mounted it in the corner, and I paid the least attention to that one.

~

That afternoon, all the cousins were called inside to watch Uncle Gavin inject Nana's knees. He gave B12 shots in the den and cortisone shots in the kitchen, where light was better for watching the needle go in. While Uncle Gavin was snapping open his doctor's bag that day, he mentioned there was a big search on for the missing State Trooper, and they had called people in from Knoxville to help. When I thought about the burlap sack in the tadpole pond and the gravel crunching on the Florist Shop Road, my head started turning. When I imagined Clyne gouging all our eyes out, I thought about hiding in the cedar closet behind the bed where I could climb underneath the pile of quilts and lay stock still if I had to. My mother and Nana would be waiting in their rooms, not knowing what Clyne had in store. I didn't know what to do.

When I came into the kitchen, Nana pulled up a chair and patted it, wanting me to sit beside her, just like she did on tube swallowing mornings.

Oh, honey. I was waiting for you and wasn't going to let Gavin give me that old needle until you were sitting right here beside me.

I don't know why Nana thought I wanted to see her knees injected. I didn't. I didn't want to be a doctor like Uncle Gavin. I wanted to sit in the den and listen to the adults discuss Nana's knees then write down what they said on my yellow pad.

She's up there mashing those pedals every night at the funeral home with knees the size of footballs.

In constant pain, constant. She was out there this morning, bending over pulling weeds.

Dinah D. Matthews, Uncle Andy said. He imitated Nana speaking to the State Trooper. *Oh, Officer. I was hurrying over to the church to drop my slaw off then I have a service to play at the funeral home.*

She had that State Trooper crawling on his hands and knees, picking up deviled eggs, and potato salad that was lying all over the interstate.

On her way to the dad gum church picnic.

Potato salad all over the interstate, Andy? Dear God in heaven. Did that happen? Potato salad?

My mother already knew it had been potato salad. Uncle Andy didn't care if my mother pretended that she didn't know something. I didn't care either but sometimes held my breath when my mother people pleased. I knew it was hell on earth for her.

The adults loved to tell stories about Nana running stop lights because of her swollen knees. All the policemen knew who she was and always let her go because she took too long trying to find her driver's license. She took everything out of her purse, one item at a time and put it all on the front seat, even pieces of Kleenex that had boogs on them.

They just let her go. She once gave a State Trooper her church card instead of her driver's license, and he let her go.

She can hardly make it down the aisle of the church then gets up on that organ bench and starts mashing those pedals.

Nana played the organ at the Church on Sunday morning then for Maggot's Funeral Home every other night of the week.

Every time she pushes down on a pedal you can see the poor thing jump. I can't stand to watch her play.

'Rodney, your Uncle Gavin has to push that old needle all the way to the bone.'

At every family reunion, when it came time for Nana to

receive her cortisone injection, we moved into the kitchen. Everybody became quiet when the needle slid into the center of Nana's knee. She puffed out her cheeks and gripped her thigh as tight as she could with both hands when Uncle Gavin pushed the needle all the way down to the hub. The cousins and the adults watched the needle back out, go in, back out and go in. Nana's mouth formed the letter O when the needle went in and clamped her lips together when it backed out.

"Lawsie mercy, Gavin has to work that old needle all the way to the bone. I know he has to do it that way to get the medicine in but Lawsie Mercy!"

Gavin told us that Nana's arthritis was so bad, her bones were touching.

Gavin has never seen knees that bad in all his years of practice.

"I could feel that old needle scraping against the bone when he was working it around."

Nana hooked her finger and pretended to scrape.

She's playing the funeral home tonight, in agony with every note.

"He has to work it around and work it around, right down by that old bone."

Nana spoke in her deep voice when Uncle Gavin worked the needle around. She looked at each cousin one by one as if she was watching us eat. The cousins stood up on their tiptoes to watch the needle get worked around.

"I know that hurts," Uncle Gavin told Nana when he was finished, then shook his head from side to side and laughed. Nana bit her lip and puffed out her cheeks again.

After cortisone shots, Nana usually sliced the Angel Food cake and one of the cousins went down to the basement to fetch a gallon of Neapolitan ice cream from the freezer. When we started eating the ice cream, my mother usually started the story of Nana falling, breaking her hip and having to crawl across the house to the phone.

When they took her to the hospital, they pinned her hip with no anesthesia. No anesthesia. Nothing. Uh huh. The doctor asked her, 'are you sure you don't want something for pain? Let us give you something.' Uh huh. Nothing. Refused.

Mother, do you remember that drain they stuck through the side of your cheek? They left that tube in there for months. Months. She nearly died and was in agony, day and night.

She went to church with it in.

"Oh it wasn't in there all that long," Nana said.

With the back of her hand, Nana pushed the centerpiece to one side and watched the cousins eat ice cream and Angel Food.

~

I didn't want to leave the bed or leave my room or think about the tadpole pond or what I hadn't said. Being awake was as bad as being asleep. I could change my nightmares most of the time, so I decided I would take my chances staying asleep. Staying asleep was safer.

I flipped the pillow onto its cool side as soon as I woke up and looked across the driveway at the streetlamp. The bugs had been tapping and tapping and tapping against its glass right before I found myself walking in the middle of the same street, passing the same sidewalk and rounding the same corner to stand in front of the same white gate as I had so many times before. The only nightmare I was not able to change was the one I had last night although the good thing about it was by the time I found myself in front of the little house, the dream was already over.

Each time I walked down that street, I never examined the houses behind their white picket fences because I couldn't turn my head to do so. Out of the corner of my eye, the houses sat side by side, and all looked the same, as if I passed the same house every few steps. As I walked up the middle of that street, I never worried but knew as soon as I strolled around the corner and saw the little house in the middle of the road, it was all going to happen again, the same way it did before. While I was on the street with the white picket fences and houses all the same, I was safe. It would all happen when I found myself standing in front of the same little house in the middle of the same street, with flower beds under its two windows, exactly where it had been in the last dream. The little house looked like it should be sitting in the middle of the woods, not in the middle of a street. More odd than that though was its little white fence looked to be closer to the house than it should have been. That was my clue. Something was off. Nobody would put a fence that close to their house.

I walked up the gate, stood and waited until my head started swimming, remembering what happened the last time I had stood in front of the gate and knowing what was just about to happen. That's when I always began to shout but couldn't breathe or move. The house had already turned into the purple thing by then, reared up and came down over my head like a wave at the ocean with me turning upside down inside of it. As soon as my head barely started to turn, the whole thing was over. The whole thing had already happened by the time I knew it was going to happen.

I got out of bed, went down to the kitchen still remembering everything about the street and the little house and how it swallowed me whole. Shaw was already downstairs eating his Cream of Wheat. Aunt Adair sat between Uncle Andy and my mother, all of them laughing. Nana beat batter in a bowl with a wooden spoon, and all I could hear was *clack clack clack*.

I didn't know why it was always the same street, and why the same thing happened the same way each time or how I knew it was going to happen that way and there was nothing I could do to stop it.

13
AUNT SCOBIE, PEPTO BISMOL, AND BASEBALL CARDS

When Shaw whispered to me across the table about the new dare, I felt like we were in a huddle and Shaw was Joe Namath. I was Emerson Boozer, the running back.

"Listen here. Roddoh, you cut through the woods on the other side of the sandbox into Uncle Jerry and Aunt Scobie's yard. Then you pick up one of her snakes and bring it back."

Shaw said he was going back home soon and needed to fit in a few good dares for me. Aunt Adair heard Shaw give me the dare and said, "You boys are not to bother Old Aunt Scobie. She's out of her mind."

Old Aunt Scobie lived with Uncle Jerry in the house next door on the other side of woods beyond the sandbox. My mother said,

"I would NOT go back into those woods. May sleeps back in there. I know she does because Munro's told me he's found her back in there. Were she to knife one of you. . . MM mm."

Nana said, "Oh, Rindy Anne, HUSH. No one sleeps back in there."

My mother then said: "Uncle Jerry's a BIG alcoholic, you know."

She had been talking about Old May then began talking about Uncle Jerry. Nana shushed my mother because she didn't want the cousins to know Old May had bowel movements in our sandbox. The cousins already knew more about Old May's bowel movements than Nana did.

We also knew Aunt Scobie laid out rubber snakes in her front yard to scare children away. What Aunt Scobie didn't know was that rubber snakes didn't work with children: Children loved to play with rubber snakes. If Nana handed me pocket change and dropped me off at the Five-and-Dime, a rubber snake would be at the top of my list. Shaw said Aunt Scobie had a rattlesnake, a copperhead, a boa constrictor, a garter snake, a python and the black snake. I wondered whether Uncle Jerry bought them for her or if Old Aunt Scobie went into the Five-and-Dime herself. I had a rubber copperhead and a coral snake; that was it.

Duncan told me he saw Shaw swing Aunt Scobies's black snake around and around over his head but didn't know old Aunt Scobie had been watching him out of her living room window. Adair had been standing right behind Aunt Scobie and had to shout out the window for Shaw to put the snake down. That's why Shaw had made it a dare; he had already been caught doing it. Shaw did most of them himself then dared the other cousins to do the same. Aunt Scobie's snake dare was considered a medium.

My mother said: "Andy, Gavin, and I would go over to visit and Aunt Scobie would all of a sudden rise out of her chair and go *UHHAHHHHHH*. She would be sitting there then just go *UHHAHHHHH*. One time Andy turned and looked straight at Gavin and I. He didn't smile, just looked at us right after she did that. He didn't have to say a word. We started laughing and couldn't stop. Scobie was getting the best dope in town from Dr. Presley. I don't know what it was he was giving her, but it was the best."

Uncle Andy said, "The best dope in town."

"And she hates children, HATES them! That's why you can't go over there by yourself. She may even have a gun under her living room sofa to shoot at children in her front yard. She's that far gone."

I didn't know why my mother said Aunt Scobie hated children. She had already told me Aunt Scobie *acts* like she hates children but doesn't hate them.

She's AFRAID of children. Aunt Scobie and Uncle Jerry don't have them, you see. They couldn't or Aunt Scobie didn't want them, I'm not sure which but because of that, Aunt Scobie doesn't understand children and never did. Children scare her.

"She sits over there, watching cartoons all day long, high as a kite," Adair said.

I thought Aunt Scobie was one of the most interesting people I had ever known. I wanted to examine her while she watched cartoons more than examining anything else in the world. If Dad was in Tennessee, I know he would want to examine her as well. Dad and I watched cartoons together in New York when he was in the apartment. He would come into the living room and sit on the couch if either Popeye or Wile E Coyote was on.

"Uncle Jerry doesn't mind children. I think he wanted them. He's very rich. He was all business, you see. All three brothers owned coal land that their daddy Hi Ho Magnus Matthews bought with money he earned as a miner. Seventy years in the coal mines, yes sir. But all the miners loved my daddy and he loved them."

I had already heard all the stories about my grandfather's two brothers Uncle Jerry and Uncle Henry.

Each of them had more money than daddy did. I don't know why they had more, but it had something to do with business. Something wasn't right. There was no giving within our family for one thing. No giving, only selling. Going into business with your family is hell, a living hell. Uncle Henry was very grand and felt above all the rest of us. He moved out of the mountains into a big house in Knoxville. Dixie and I had to wear white gloves whenever we visited him, beautiful white gloves.

Nobody said anything for a minute then my mother blurted out: "Uncle Jerry's toes turned blue last year. I think he had to have two of them taken off."

After my mother said that, Shaw nudged me. "C'mon." We slipped down the hallway and out the front door, ran past the sandbox and straight into the woods. All that was in my head was grabbing one of Aunt Scobie's snakes and bringing it back to my room. I ran as fast as I could through the trees and bushes letting the leaves and branches whip me because I couldn't stop with Clyne on the loose. I wasn't afraid of running into Old May because I had watched her walk down the driveway after delivering the Press, turn onto Tennessee Avenue and head toward town.

I ran full speed out into the middle of Aunt Scobie's yard before I noticed Uncle Jerry standing in his driveway across the grass. He waved. Shaw, still in the woods, whispered to me from behind a tree: "I'm going back. He's just going to show us the electric garbage can."

Always be sure to ask Uncle Jerry to show you his electric garbage can. He invented it himself and is very proud. I always make a big deal out of it every time I see him.

Shaw was right. I had already seen the electric garbage can and didn't want to see it again. Uncle Jerry put his garbage can on a hook inside his garage and flipped a switch. The garage door rose up, and the can moved outside on its track all the way down to the end of the driveway. The garbage man emptied the can, put it back on its hook, the can traveled all the way back into the garage and the garage door then closed. The whole show took twenty one minutes. I knew that because I had stood beside Uncle Jerry and watched the garbage can move out then move back in while he timed it precisely on his pocket watch. My mother told me I had to watch the whole show to make Uncle Jerry happy.

If you ever go over there, you have to watch the whole show and be sure to tell him how much you enjoyed watching it.

Uncle Jerry wanted to run the garbage can out a second time right after the first, but the whole thing had been so boring I lied to him about my feeling of having to vomit.

This time, Uncle Jerry said, "I've got a nice big pitcher of lemonade in the house, Rodney, but I was fixing to run that garbage can out. If you wanted to watch, that would be ok."

I didn't say no. I didn't say anything because we were going into the house afterward where Aunt Scobie was watching cartoons. I already heard them blaring through their living room window: Daffy Duck was on. I stood in the garage beside Uncle Jerry, and we watched the garbage can move out to the curb. This took nine minutes and thirty seconds.

"That's a new world record," Uncle Jerry said and snapped his pocket watch closed. "I'm going to stop it right there. You'll miss out on it coming back in, but I'll have to do some work on its chain if I'm going to improve that time."

I had never been happier in my whole life when Uncle Jerry stopped his electric garbage in the middle of the show and led me into the kitchen where we heard the cartoons even louder, and right across the hallway. Through the living room door, I could see the TV by the window along with the back of Aunt Scobie's head. She sat on the couch laughing her head off, shaking a finger at Daffy Duck and speaking to him.

"Don't do that," she said.

Examining Aunt Scobie while she spoke to her television set turned out to be the most fascinating thing I had ever done in my life and made every minute of watching the garbage can worth it ten times over.

All the cousins knew Old Aunt Scobie laughed at cartoons and talked back to her television, but few had ever been standing right behind her while she was doing it.

Uncle Jerry told me: "She's ok as long as she's watching cartoons but I don't let children in the house when cartoons aren't on."

Uncle Jerry talked to me as if I was one of the adults. I drank my lemonade and stood in the hallway watching the back of Aunt Scobie's head while she spoke angrily to Daffy Duck, slashing her hand through the air. After slashing, she threw a piece of sucking candy at the television screen. I was very disappointed when Uncle Jerry led me back into the kitchen for more lemonade as Old Aunt Scobie was by that time getting angrier and angrier at Daffy Duck. I stood by the sink and sipped my drink as slowly and quietly as I could so as to listen to everything Aunt Scobie was saying:

"Never do that. NEVER do that again. You just make me so mad, you SHIT, you little SHIT!"

Uncle Jerry knew I wanted to watch Aunt Scobie watch cartoons and let me do it for a few minutes longer then took my glass and said he had to get back to working on his invention.

Watching Aunt Scobie might have been a dare but most likely was not because Uncle Jerry had invited me into their house. If I had to sneak in and hide, then it would have been a full dare and considered a big one.

I still ran full speed back into the woods the way we had come, and couldn't wait to tell Shaw everything that had happened.

~

As soon as I caught sight of Kezia Willoughby through the leaves, I grabbed hold of a tree branch to stop from running out into the clearing. She knelt on the ground with Clyne pushing and pulling her. I took one step backward onto a stick. It cracked, and I froze as still as a statue.

Kezia's head turned, and I could see her teeth sticking straight out of her mouth pointing at me. Her eyes were slits, like a snake's, but I couldn't be sure they were closed. She gripped the edge of the sandbox with both hands. Her shirt was pulled all the way up and her big titties were out, covered in white sand. I watched them roll back and forth every time Clyne pushed and pulled her. If Duncan had been there, he would have nudged me and said:

Oh my God, Roddoh, look at her big titties!

They were searching the county high and wide for Clyne and there he was, smack in front of me, right beside the cousins' sandbox, snorting through his nose behind Kezia Willoughby. Taking one step at a time, I walked backward through the woods and didn't know if either Clyne or Kezia had heard the stick crack or had seen me standing there and hoped more than anything in the world that they hadn't. By peeking at them through the leaves, I had qualified for a see-no-evil. When I had tiptoed far enough and could no longer see the sandbox, I stood stock still for another moment and listened but only heard Clyne's snorting. I turned and began to walk but stopped after a few steps and lifted my shoe. The brown doo caked both sides of the sole. My Ked had sliced straight down the middle of a large dook laying in the middle of a maple leaf, the worst thing that could have happened at that moment.

Old May had laid her snake on a booby-trapped silver platter for me to step on. The dook was wet and smelled so strong that I peered through the breaks in the trees one more time to make sure she hadn't looped back from town and was lurking in the woods, observing the spot where she laid her snake down. I picked up a stick and started pushing the dook off then turned my knee out, wiped my sole against the bark of a pine then began rubbing it back and forth over the leaves on the ground.

Bobwhite bobwhite bob bob bob bob.

I stopped rubbing to listen for another bobwhite to answer but instead heard a *crack* somewhere deep in the woods, turned and started running as fast as I could with dook still on the bottom of my shoe. I came out beside Nana's greenhouse and made a beeline for the house. The cousins were all sitting at the kitchen table playing Spades. I wasn't going to say anything to anybody about what I'd seen, and hopped straight past them into the hallway, hopped into the downstairs bathroom and rinsed the bottom of my shoe under the bathtub faucet.

When I finally sat down on my bed, I looked at my bag of green army men and then to the old photograph propped up on the polyurethaned dresser: Tootsie and Laddy, the two chief Toy Manchesters, had been coming up the driveway under the dogwoods. Kezia's titties had looked like two loaves of Wonder bread. Her eyes had narrowed when her head turned. I didn't want her eyes to have been open but thought they might have been and that she had not only seen me but had watched me watch Clyne pushing and pulling her from behind.

I felt like it was all going to come out in my pants and walked very slow on my heels into the bathroom to look for the Pepto Bismol. Nana kept both Pepto Bismol and Halley's MO in the upstairs bathroom cabinet. I liked Pepto Bismol.

Nana liked her Haley's MO better than Pepto Bismol. Haley's MO made me want to vomit. Nana poured a teaspoon of whiskey and mixed it in with a teaspoon of Haley's MO every time a cousin came down with a cold.

Run and fetch me the Haley's MO.

I was always glad to run and get the Haley's MO but only if Nana or Marjorie or Munro were taking it, not me.

When I went into the bathroom and opened the cabinet, the first thing I saw was the bottle of camphor. Nana dabbed camphor on everything. We didn't have camphor in New York. We had Bacteen.

I had been bitten by a bug the day Old May jumped out at us, and my arm swelled up to the size of a football. My mother put Calamine on then Nana came into the kitchen with her bottle of camphor and said,

See here, Rodney, lend me your arm right quick and let me put some of this good camphor on it.

My arm was better by that afternoon because of the camphor, but I smelled like I was living inside a bottle of it all that night and all the next day.

I took the Pepto Bismol out of the medicine cabinet and swigged it. My mother always told me to *Just swig it straight out of the bottle.*

~

Clyne was still not only out there; he was everywhere.

After swigging from the bottle of Pepto Bismol, it began sprinkling outside. I sat on the side of my bed and listened to rain tapping the gravel in the driveway.

I took out my suitcase from under the bed, removed all my baseball cards and spread them out on the bed. I had brought down Mickey Mantle to show John Bass. I had one Mickey Mantle, one Yogi Berra, and one Whitey Ford up in New York, but didn't risk bringing all three.

Duncan told me his friends only liked the Braves or the Cardinals but that he didn't care about baseball. Duncan loved the Green Bay Packers more than any other team in the world. Duncan had Packers pennants on his wall, a Packers lamp by his bed and Packers sheets. He had a poster of Bart Starr on the back of his door.

Green Bay, Roddoh! Oh my God, Green Bay!

Duncan bit his lip whenever the Packers were playing and always had his Packers jacket on the day before and the day of a game.

Each time my mother said you got a letter from Duncan, I held it up to the light to see the stick of Juicy Fruit inside. Nobody in the Post Office ever opened Duncan's letter to take the Juicy Fruit out. I was always surprised about that because you could see it was Juicy Fruit. Each time I read one of Duncan's letters, I had already unwrapped the stick and would be chewing it.

I decided to give Duncan my Ray Nitschke, not just show it to him. I brought Mickey Mantle to show John Bass, not give to him because John liked the Braves, not the Yankees and it would have been a waste of a Mickey Mantle.

I brought down Bobby Orr since he was hockey and they didn't have hockey in Tennessee. I loved the Bruin's black and gold uniform more than any other. I also packed Vic Hadfield, Rod Gilbert, and Terry Sawchuk and slipped Gordie Howe in the suitcase at the last second.

I took out all the Yankees, which, except for Mickey Mantle, were all doubles: Joe Pepitone, Horace Duncan, Gene Michael, Steve Whitaker and Fritz Peterson. I had three Al Downings and three Bill Monbouquettes in New York and brought one of each. After the Yankees, I took out the Mets. I kept those two teams separate. I brought the Mets down in my suitcase side pocket. I had a Tom Seaver, a Bud Harrelson, a Tommy Agee, a Ron Swoboda, a Tug Mcgraw and an Ed Kranepool. I had two Gary Gentrys, four Art Shamskys and a lot of Duffy Dyers up in New York.

After the Mets, I got out my Tigers and laid Mickey Lolich on the bed, then lined up Norm Cash, Mickey Stanley, Jim Northrup and Willie Horton to one side of him. I liked the Detroit Tigers probably more than anybody in New York City. Every year Uncle Thomas sent me a Detroit Tigers program, and I read every page over and over.

Uncle Thomas used to have a big thing about me and wanted me to marry him even though I was married to Dad. He still has a thing for me after all these years. He's trying to get to me through you.

I didn't care about Uncle Thomas' thing, and Dad didn't care either. Last year Uncle Thomas sent me a real Louisville Slugger signed by Al Kaline. It was a thirty-two. Uncle Gavin looked at it when he was visiting us in New York and said,

That's the real McCoy.

The last card I took out was my Brooks Robinson. He was almost my favorite; maybe was my favorite. I had been watching TV the one night he made a sideways catch at third base, and I couldn't stop clapping and yelling just like Dad clapped and yelled and stood up in the living room when Rod Laver won Wimbledon.

I had borrowed my mother's transistor radio when the Cardinals beat the Tigers ten to one in Game 4 of the World Series. I had also been listening when the Tigers beat the Cardinals thirteen to one in Game 6. When Jim Northrup hit the grand slam, I clapped and screamed and jumped up and down for five full minutes. In the last game, Norm Cash and Willie Horton hit singles in the seventh inning, then Jim Northrup hit a triple, and it looked like it was going to be the Tigers. I jumped to my feet but didn't scream. The game wasn't over, so I kept standing. When the Tigers won, I yelled like Dad and couldn't control myself. I listened to the crowd screaming over my transistor and screamed along with them.

By the time I had finished looking at all my cards, the sky was the color of Nana's cast iron skillet. Thunder and lightning came.

I heard Munro's truck start, and after he had pulled away, I didn't feel that I was going to have diarrhea. I wasn't sure if Clyne had ridden home in his daddy's truck after busting the middle Willoughby sister out by our sandbox. I didn't think he would have and figured Munro probably didn't even suspect Clyne was anywhere near Nana's house with everybody in East Tennessee out looking for him.

A few minutes after the truck pulled away, the sky got bright and blossomed like a white flower outside my window. The *CRACK,* right after that, made me jump.

We only had stick lightning in New York, but Tennessee had three kinds. One was ball lightning. Nana told me ball lightning came through Joann Sharp's front door one day while she was cleaning her refrigerator.

She watched it move down the hallway, turn into the kitchen and sit up on top of her stove. Joann isn't the kind of person that would make something like that up. When it got into her kitchen, she said the ball lightning was so still that it looked to be thinking about something right before it shot off into her pantry.

The other kind of lightning besides stick was *heat lightning.* Whenever the weather turned hot without rain, heat lightning hung over the mountains. I liked to tell Nana whenever I spotted it. Heat lightning looked like someone had lit a blanket on fire then shook it. The sky flickered all the way across and you didn't hear thunder.

There's heat lightning over there, Nana.

Why, yes, look at that pretty heat lightning over yonder.

14
SOCKS, MULE PULLING, AND THE FILLING STATIONS

Munro came to the back door the next morning to take Duncan and me over to watch the Tennessee Walking Horses train at the barn on the edge of town. I told him I wasn't feeling good and would be staying in the house, but Duncan was still going. Munro tilted his hat back and looked at his hands.

"I don't know if you heard, but Clyne went down to Knoxville and joined the Marine Corps yesterday."

I had never been happier in my entire life the moment when Munro told me the Marines had taken Clyne.

"He wants that anchor and globe is what he wants." Munro cupped his hands over his forearm, chuckled, then reached up and shifted his cap back and forth. "They took him straight off and put him on the bus to boot camp. They're making him sergeant from what I hear." Munro gazed at the sun. "He'll be stepping off that bus in Paris Island, South Carolina right about now."

I returned to the kitchen table, picked up my bowl and tilted it, trying to pour as much Cream of Wheat in my open mouth as I could then ran down the hallway, out the front door, jumped off the porch and slid in the gravel about three feet. I couldn't wait to see the Walking Horses. Clyne had joined the Marines!

Whenever Munro gave us a ride, we'd pick up a man named Socks, who lived in a little white trailer way out on the Loop. Socks took care of all the Walkers over at the barn.

I looked out the truck window at the passing trees, thinking about what Munro had told me and that Clyne had said the same thing, that they were making him a sergeant. I wondered how that could be true that the Marines would make him a sergeant as soon as he joined. I wondered how Clyne could have gotten over to Knoxville and on a bus to Paris Island so quickly after he'd been busting Kezia Willoughby over our sandbox the day before and hadn't looked like he was in any hurry. I didn't care what the reason was; I was just glad Clyne was getting off the bus in Paris Island right about now. They could make him a Five Star General his very first day. I didn't care. He was gone. I was enjoying my ride in Munro's truck that morning more than any truck or car ride I had ever taken in my life.

Munro's truck had a pull start and radio over the cigarette lighter. Munro had let me start it the summer before, and I had never forgotten what that felt like. I wanted to start it again more than anything in the world, but Munro had told me:

"I'll let you do this once, and only once."

Right after Munro started his truck, he pushed in his cigarette lighter then turned on the radio. He smoked his Winstons whenever he drove his truck and always hung his arm out the window holding the burning cigarette. Munro's truck crunched when he jerked the gear shift. He explained the clutch and the gear shifting to me the day he let me start the truck and had also pointed out the different radio stations. Each time we rode in Munro's truck, we listened to some of the same songs over and over.

Well, my daddy left home when I was three and didn't leave much for ma and me 'cept this ole guitar and an empty bottle of booze.

When the men in the audience cheered, I cheered like the men. The cheering audience was part of that song.

These boots are made for walkin' and that's just what they'll do and one of these days these boots are gonna walk all over you dih doo dih dih doo.

When Munro turned on the radio this morning, we heard: "Like a Rhinestone Cow-boy."

Duncan screamed out, *like a rhinestone RHINESTONE!* And we laughed our heads off. Even Munro smiled.

This time, on the way to Socks' house, Duncan said, "Socks doesn't have a car because he wrecked it driving *rnnt.*"

I hadn't known what *rnnt* meant the first time I heard Duncan say it so I had asked Marjorie.

Ruined. Some people say rnnt for drunkenness.

Marjorie always answered my questions if she could, and I asked her questions I didn't ask anybody else. I almost told her about the tadpole pond but didn't want to get her into trouble. Telling her might have. After Marjorie had explained what *rnnt* meant, I had gone into the downstairs bathroom and practiced the different ways I had heard people say it:

Rnnt! He's rnnt! Perseus comes to work RNNT every day, and Nana doesn't even know. Perseus is rnnt. He's up there rnnt this minute.

Munro drove us out onto the Loop then down a brown dirt road past a field beside a fence tangled up in rusty barbed wire with all its posts leaning over to one side. Munro knew exactly where to find Socks' scuffed up white trailer sitting behind a grove of ragweed, right on the edge of the woods. Munro beeped his horn when he pulled up. If Socks wasn't in his trailer, Munro always knew where to find him. I didn't know how he knew. This morning, Socks came out in his overalls and boots.

"Oh my God, Roddoh. There's Socks!" Duncan said.

"Socks," I said.

"Ole Socks. When you see him, ask him what he wants for breakfast. Ask him, Roddoh."

Duncan had told me that Socks had been a Marine in Viet Nam and had to eat bugs and snakes in the jungle for nearly a month after they had left him out there by mistake. Duncan said that after Socks came back, he didn't care whether he was eating salamanders or meatloaf, that it didn't make any difference to him. I didn't want to ask Socks what he wanted for breakfast after hearing that.

When Socks climbed into Munro's truck, I looked at the writing on his arm and turned my head to try and read the waterfall of words from his shoulder to hand. Socks had them tattooed on in Saigon. The words meant something but nobody knew what. Socks' arm was as mysterious as a page out of *The Arabian Nights* and I couldn't stop looking at it.

When Socks climbed into Munro's truck, he smelled like one of Nana's grilled hot dogs. Nana grilled hot dogs in her iron skillet, used butter and cooked them until they almost turned black. After I had smelled Socks, I turned around and smelled Munro. Munro smelled like a filling station gas pump.

I was so happy that Clyne was in the Marines that I thought about how much I loved sniffing gas whenever Nana pulled into the Texaco station and how the gas smelled so much better at Texaco than at Sinclair. I also noticed the blood on Munro's chin.

Munro spits up blood, my mother told me. Munro had tuberculosis and sometimes came to the back door for a swig of Nana's Bayer's Emulsion.

Mrs. Matthews, I'm sick.

Marjorie, run get the Bayer's emulsion.

Dear God. Mother gives Munro Bayer's Emulsion for his tuberculosis.

Uncle Gavin always laughed when my mother mentioned that. Nana kept Bayer's Emulsion only in the downstairs bathroom.

I don't even know if they make it any longer, Rindy. She must have had that bottle of Bayer's Emulsion since civil defense. I think it's got opium in it.

My mother loved imitating Nana talking about Munro's

TB.

There's nothing wrong with Munro. Just run get the Bayer's emulsion.

Mother, Munro is spitting up blood.

People say that Munro has the TB, but we don't know if that's true. I don't think it's true. If you see him spit up blood, just don't let it get on your shoes.

"Socks, what do you want for breakfast?" Duncan asked.

Socks started speaking "*Hep hep hephephep.*" He said *quart* this, *quart* that and *goddamn quart*.

Socks was from way up in the mountains of Eastern Kentucky but he's a lot smarter than you think he is and half the time he's messing with you.

Munro stopped his truck at the Top Hat and ordered Socks a quart at the drive through window.

I said "Quart" then "Goddamn quart" and didn't think anybody was listening but turned my head to find Socks staring straight at me. I couldn't be sure if he was smiling. He looked like someone had Scotch-taped his lips closed. He kept staring at me and I started to get worried when, all of a sudden, Socks cracked his fingers like a whip, grinned then turned his head away and kept looking out the truck window.

When we got to the barn, Socks began talking to himself like Old May. He nailed a shoe onto a Tennessee Walker's hoof and spoke so quickly that he sounded like the auctioneer at High Clabbie Clappers. He lifted the horse's leg and moved it around as if it were a piece of wood and even though he was sitting right behind the horse's rear end, Socks never looked worried that he might get kicked.

Socks knew what caused the Walking Horses to lift their legs up and throw them out, which was called *coming up*. The horses didn't know how to come up when they were born, but in the shows, they picked their legs way up, threw them out as if being ridden by kings and queens.

Socks shouted *comup* at the young ones and followed them around the barn making sure they came up with each step. If they didn't, he tied a chain around their ankles, rubbed a little bit of acid underneath, then scrubbed the spot with a stick. He whacked the back of their legs with an even longer stick while they walked. He did this until they came up with every step. The younger horses didn't like the acid or chains and bucked and threw flying side-kicks at Socks. The Walkers were as fast as Mr. Chun in his Tai Kwon Do studio in New York but Socks knew how to get out of their way in time.

After he had fixed the shoe on the black horse, Socks gave Munro his quart to hold. While Munro was taking a few swigs, Socks jumped into his truck and began following that same Walker around the ring outside, ramming him from behind and screaming *COMUP* out the window.

When Munro saw what Socks was doing, he yelled at the top of his lungs for him to get out of his truck. Socks pretended like he didn't hear Munro and kept spinning the wheels and swerving from side to side.

"You goddamn motherfucker Socks! That's my goddamn motherfucking truck, goddamn son of a bitch yew!"

I said, "son of a bitch yew," but not loud enough for anybody to hear.

"Ole Munro!" Duncan said. "Roddoh, you can hit a Walking Horse real hard with a truck, and it won't hurt it. Little by little, though, it learns to come up."

~

Knowing that Clyne was in Paris Island, I was excited to see the mule pulling at the County Fair with Duncan that night. When we pulled in, all the lights from the tops of the rides and inside the concession stands made the fairgrounds look like Macy's at Christmas. People had driven all the way down from Kentucky and the field by the entrance was filled with cars. The very first thing Duncan and I did was buy a crushed cherry icy. We carried them over to an old concrete ramp to watch a man in overalls and an orange Gulf cap harness two white mules onto a sled.

"That's the puller," Duncan said.

My head jerked when the lady in the announcer's platform blew her whistle over the loudspeaker. Two black mules right behind us started straining and jerking on their load of cinder blocks. Their puller didn't have sleeves on his shirt, wore an Alcoa cap and jerked the reigns, hopping from leg to leg, up and down, like he was being shocked to death, yelling: "getupmyooulgetupmtooyulgetupmyooyul."

The lady tooted her whistle again and two men with big

bellies, one wearing a blue Ford cap, the other an orange Chevy, unhooked the load. The puller stood on the sled and let his two black mules pull him away as if he was water skiing.

"That was a good pull for Eugene Deckers," the lady announced.

The puller we had already seen over by the concrete ramp led his two white mules over to the men with big bellies who added more cinder blocks to the load, attached his sled and the lady blew her whistle. This puller didn't hop up and down but followed his mules slapping the reigns and yelling: "IkeyMikeyIkeyMikeyIkeyMikey" at the top of his lungs then "Whoa."

"Another good pull for James Heatherly," the lady announced, and I had time to take a bite out of my crushed cherry icy.

People were walking everywhere at the Mule Pulling, more people in one place than I had ever seen in Tennessee. The floodlights made the clouds stand out as if they been drawn on the sky and we were all standing inside a fish bowl looking through its glass. Duncan pointed to a girl leaning against an old green tractor and said,

"Oh my God, Roddoh. There's Barn Woman. She's one nice big hot plate of pussy."

I didn't have hairs yet, so I didn't know what to think about a nice big hot plate of pussy and pretended to laugh.

Duncan pumped his arm and said, "I could use a nice big hot plate of pussy!"

Both Duncan and Shaw knew about hot plates of pussy and had mentioned them to me before. Barn Woman wore a cowboy hat and had been watching a man with an Army cap yank down on a harness strap then buckle it.

"I just want to be knee deep in that. Look at it, Roddoh!"

Duncan had hairs, so all he thought about was being knee deep in hot plates of pussy.

"Oh my God, look at Barn Woman, Roddoh," Duncan said. "We need to get you some of that pussy."

When Duncan told me he was going to get me some of that pussy, I started worrying again. Clyne had joined the Marines, but I still had Old May and Tube Swallowing along with the bodies left in the tadpole pond to worry about. I wasn't sure if I wanted a nice big hot plate of pussy, especially if the hot plate of pussy had hairs and I didn't. I decided I didn't want to be knee deep in a hot plate of pussy without hairs.

"Roddoh, I'm going to get you a nice big hot plate of pussy before you get back up there to New York."

I needed hairs and needed them quick. I hoped they would come in before Duncan got me the hot plate of pussy but didn't think they would. When there was an emergency, I prayed. This situation was an emergency so I prayed silently to God that my hairs would come in.

Duncan asked me, "Do you want to get some pussy?"

I said, "OK, pussy."

"Pussy, Roddoh," Duncan said.

"Pussy," I said.

"Oh my god, there's Barn Woman, Roddoh. Just look at it," Duncan said. I had to remember to write down what Duncan was saying about pussy when I got back to my room. I looked over at Barn Woman's cowgirl boots then at her boobs pushing out her cowgirl shirt then up into the sky, the clouds as sharp as if they had been cut with a knife.

"She puts out," Duncan said. "Barn Woman works the horses. She's sixteen but look at her, Roddoh. Barn Woman is wild. She's wild."

I examined Barn Woman and had to place one hand over my forehead like an awning to see her clearly as she stood near a flood light. Barn Woman looked like Raquel Welch and I know had more than a few hairs. Duncan told me he was going to ask Barn Woman to set me up with one of her friends and told me we would all go to the drive-in movie together. Duncan had his farm permit so he could take Uncle Gavin's LTD or my mother's Comet. Duncan told me Barn Woman would be sitting in the front seat, and the girl and I would be sitting in the back.

"Barn Woman's got a big ole bush, Roddoh," Duncan said.

I would be the only one in the car who didn't have hairs. I didn't want to be in the backseat of the car if I didn't have hairs. Duncan told me the girl who was going to sit with me in the back seat was a full twelve, had titties and a bush, just like I thought she might. Now I had to worry about the girl's bush at the same time worrying about tube swallowing and Old May stabbing me to death. And like

Old May stabbing me to death, I didn't know when the setting-up in the back seat was going to happen.

The girl I wanted to sit beside was Ginger Rose. I didn't care if she had a bush or not. When I fished at Rose's dock, Ginger Rose was always there. Her daddy owned it. She worked at the concession stand and knew a lot about motorboats and houseboats. I had seen Ginger Rose every single summer since I had been coming down to Tennessee.

Ginger Rose was asking her mother, 'When is Rodney coming down? When is Rodney coming down?' That's all she asks. She always asks when you'll be coming down again. I think she has a big thing about you, a BIG thing.

I watched Ginger Rose whenever she was nearby but couldn't say more than a single word to her. Ginger Rose always looked at me like she was standing at the church door, handing me a program. She looked straight into my eyes and seemed glad I was there. No one else seemed as glad to see me as Ginger Rose. She kept watching me just like I kept watching her. I listened to her talk and listened to her laugh. She was at the Sand Lake swimming pool every time I went over with my mother, and I liked it she was there, but couldn't say anything. I couldn't speak when Ginger Rose was around.

Ginger Rose ran fast as any boy and did flips off the high board. I stared at her whenever she was at the pool just as I stared at her when she walked down the length of Rose's dock. We sat side by side at the end of the dock not saying anything whenever I went over there to fish for bass.

I would rather be sitting beside Ginger Rose on Rose's

Dock than in the back seat with Barn Woman's twelve-year-old friend who had titties and a bush.

When Ginger Rose and I sat at the end of Rose's Dock to fish, you looked over the edge and kept looking. After a minute, a shape appeared. You couldn't tell what the shape was but already knew it was a bass. On some days, the bass wouldn't show up at Rose's Dock. Most of the time, it was the best place to fish for bass in the entire Norris Lake. You wet the Wonder Bread, rolled it into a little ball and slipped the hook through. If you dropped the ball of bread into the water, the bass swam up sideways, sucked in the ball and dropped back down, flickering silver and white until everything became dark green again. When you dropped the whole line into the water, you watched the ball go down until it disappeared then waited for the jerk.

The jerk and the line pulling straight with the pole bending was one of the most exciting things in the world. If the line kept jerking, you started reeling and kept looking down to see the flashing. The pole bent, and you watched the bass flashing then felt it thrashing. Finally, you pulled the fish out of the water and gauged how heavy it was on the end of the line. The bass switched back and forth and slapped the dock with its tail, bending its body up and down. I had to put my foot on the bass to get the hook out of its mouth. I liked to catch bass over and over, sometimes the same one, seeing the white flash in the dark green water and feel what that was like pulling the fish up and out over and over. I liked throwing them back, because as soon as they hit the surface, they shot off into the dark green as fast as a bullet.

Ginger Rose always asked me what I was fishing for when we met me at the end of the dock. I told her *bass*. She said *uh huh,* and that was it. I had a lot to say to Ginger Rose but never said a word other than *bass*. I didn't say a single word to her all last summer or any summer before that, except *bass*. I missed seeing her when I was in New York and always wondered what Ginger Rose was doing.

My mother always kept telling me: *Ginger Rose has a big thing about you, a BIG thing.*

My mother talked to Ginger Rose's mother and she told her that Ginger Rose had a crush on me, and that was why she asked her mother to drive her to the Sand Lake pool whenever I was there. I always bought Cheetos at the pool's concession stand and my fingers would turn yellow. I also peed in the pool when I went underwater. I liked the big pool at Sand Lake more than any pool in the world.

Ginger Rose was there the day I did a snake in the deep end. I didn't say one word to anybody but had to go so I went underwater, pushed the snake out and shook it out of my bathing suit. It floated instead of sunk. When I got out of the pool and saw my snake bobbing, I jumped back in and pushed water at it with my hand, so it floated over to the side. I got out and pretended like I didn't know it was there. Some woman saw the snake a few minutes later and told the lifeguard. She stood at the edge of the pool pointing at it until he came over with a little net. After that, they didn't let anybody in the deep end until they checked for more dook.

The next day, even the Basses had heard about someone doing a snake in the pool at Sand Lake. That someone was me.

I admitted to my mother I had been the one who did the

snake and she told me she was proud:

Good! If you can't hold it then just GO. NEVER hold it. Mother always made me hold it. 'Oh, you don't have to go. No, you don't,' she used to say. But I did. Mother was humiliated if we had to go. It's very important to let children go when they have to. I had to let it go during Mrs. Creekmore's class once. She couldn't see but the class could. Dixie was sitting right across from me as it trickled right down the center of the aisle under Mrs. Creekmore's desk. Dear God! Everybody could see the stream.

After the snake at Sand Lake, Duncan told Shaw that my mother told him Ginger Rose had a thing about me. I wished my mother had never said ANYTHING about that because now all the cousins knew.

Shaw showed me how to use pillows from my bed, fold them and make out with them, pretending it was Ginger Rose. Shaw told me kissing the pillow was a lot like kissing a girl. You folded the pillow over while you were making out and held the fold like it was the back of her head.

Shaw and Duncan both said they liked Kezia Willoughby's titties and knew why Clyne had been busting her every chance he got. Shaw also liked Herman Munster's niece and Raquel Welch. Duncan liked Raquel Welch as well. When Shaw told Duncan that Raquel Welch was on *One Million Years BC*, we all ran into Nana's room to watch it.

Raquel Welch, Roddoh! Duncan said. Oh, my GOD!

All the cousins in Nana's room to watch *One Million Years BC*. Raquel Welch played a cave man. When Raquel Welch's full head came on the screen, Shaw went right up to the TV and put his lips on Raquel Welch's lips.

The twins said, *look at what Shaw is doing to the TV*. Then Duncan said,

Look at Raquel Welch's big ole titties. That's one big hot plate of pussy!

The twins said *Duncan* at the same time. The twins were older than me by three years, and you couldn't tell them apart. They always sat beside me in the car when we went to the drive-in, and I held the popcorn that all three of us shared.

In New York, I had a babysitter from Sweden that I couldn't stop looking at, just like I couldn't stop looking at Ginger Rose. I couldn't say one word to the Swedish babysitter if she was sitting in the same room as me.

You just sit on the living room couch and stare at her, from the time we leave until the time we get back.

I didn't think I stared at her the whole time, but maybe I did.

Sex. It was all about sex in my day, you see. And the church was THE worse. They were all doing it, the minister, everybody.

I liked the nose picking stories more than the sex stories my mother would tell. My favorite was Nana picking her nose, flicking the boog with her thumb and hitting my mother in the forehead with it. My mother said everybody saw Nana do it. The boog came right off Nana's thumb, sailed across the den and hit my mother square in the middle of her forehead.

Yes! She hit me right smack in the middle of my forehead with it. Right there!

When telling that story, my mother always pointed to the middle of her forehead and told us how she felt with the boog sticking there. She told us how everybody in the family had seen it on her forehead and that Nana wouldn't even admit to flicking it.

Everybody saw it. Mother denied it. I said, 'Mother.' She said, 'Oh hush, Rindy Anne.'

My mother imitated how Nana flicked it with her thumb and flicked her thumb over and over. I understood how she knew how to imitate it so well because I had seen Nana flick her boogs when she thought nobody was looking. She flipped her thumb straight up in the air like an umpire calling a player out at home plate. Sometimes the boog hung off Nana's finger, and I had to look at it. I watched and waited to see what she did with the dangling boog. Sometimes she just let it dangle but usually flicked it away with her thumb.

~

The day after the mule pulling, Nana patted her hands on the armrests of her den chair and said, "Rodney, let's you and I go to town."

At least once every summer Nana took me to town in the Olds and introduced me to everybody she knew.

We always drove down Tennessee Avenue and stopped at the Post Office where Nana waited in line, and I looked at the recruiting brochures. I picked up one of each: Army,

Navy, Air Force and Marines. I already had a set at Nana's but loved the look of the insignias on the each brochure. Nana told me to put them all back where I found them but luckily, I had already slid one of the Air Force brochures out of sight into my back pocket. We pulled up at the Main Street intersection surrounded by the oldest buildings in town. Nana always said:

Main Street was one hundred feet wide originally which was unusual back then. They built it clear back in 1897.

People's Bank sat on the opposite corner, with a granite arch and round steel front door which made the whole building look like a big square safe. The County law offices on our side of the street were rectangles made of red brick, old and serious, with no markings other than dark stains coming down from the rooves that looked like tears. I always craned my head out the window to look at the sidewalk to see the purple stains from Saturday when farmers came into town, stood and whittled and spit out their tobacco.

You can always tell how crowded it'd been from how purple the sidewalks were on Sunday morning. On some weeks, the town has to send somebody to go over that corner with a power washer.

I could see Sheldon's Shoe store, the Five and Dime, Filene's Dress Shop, Couch's Hardware and Chippewa Movie Theater all in a row. Across the street was Rexall's, Bargain Basement and The Beauty Parlor.

Nana's first stop was always Osborne Olds, to say hello to Mr. Osborne. When we pulled into Osborne Olds, Mr. Osborne himself walked out of his showroom and said, *Well, Dinah D!* and shook Nana's hand.

Well, Jim Osborne, how yew? Oh Jim, I just want you to say hello to my grandson Rodney.

Nana had never bought a car other than an Oldsmobile and had known Mr. Osborne for years and years. Nana knew the president of People's Bank; knew Cooster Couch, who ran Couch's Hardware; and knew Mr. Griffith, who ran Griffith's Department Store. They all came outside, shook hands with Nana and said,

Well, Dinah D. Matthews!

Well, it's good to see yew. How yew?

I always waited in the Olds for them to finish the *how yew how yews.*

After Osborne Olds, we visited the bee man.

We're going to see the bee man and get you a haircut.

Nana bought fresh honey straight out of the comb from the bee man, Mr. Harold. He cut my hair on his back porch. While he was cutting, I looked out the screen at his bee boxes.

Mr. Harold goes out to his hives wearing a bee suit to get our honey. The bees cover him from head to toe. He knows how to be so calm that not a single bee will sting him.

I never once saw Mr. Harold wearing his bee suit. When he cut my hair, I imagined the bees covering him from head to toe. We never got there in time to see Mr. Harold covered with bees; he had already climbed out of the suit because Nana called ahead each time. I wanted to see Mr. Harold dressed in his bee suit and covered in bees more than anything in the world but never have and probably never will.

After the bee man, Nana drove further out to the cake lady's house to pick up an Angel Food or a Coconut for after dinner. On the way to the cake lady's house, we passed the junk yard and saw the stacks of tires.

I used to take you around just to look at tires. We would just ride around looking at tires all day long.

Every single time Nana took me to town in the Olds she said that and thought I didn't remember looking at tires with her, but I did.

Rodney, when you were about this high, you would say, 'Wheels' and I would say, 'Oh look at all the wheels, Rodney,' and you would just look and look and look and it was your favorite thing in the world to drive around and just look at the wheels.

I remembered that driving by the stack of tires in the Olds with Nana felt like heaven on earth because there was nothing to worry about then. I liked looking at truck tires the best and didn't think about anything else but tires, tires, tires and missed those days because that was all I had to think about: wheels. Nobody had been after me back then as they were now.

We went to a different filling station each trip into town. There were four of them: Esso, Texaco, Sinclair, and Mobile.

At Texaco and Sinclair, both men wore uniforms. If I had a choice between the Texaco and Sinclair, I would pick the Texaco uniform because the shirt and pants were bone white with the Texaco star over the front pocket. If I had to pick a filling station, I'd pick Sinclair. The man working at Sinclair was Buddy Tippin. He leaned on Nana's window and always took time cleaning her windshield, checking the oil and talking to both of us. I liked the dinosaur on the Sinclair sign more than the star on Texaco's.

The man who worked at Texaco was Blackie. He wore his Texaco cap and Texaco shirt but Perseus called him *the biggest asshole who ever walked the face of the Earth.* When Nana told Blackie to put High-Test in the Olds, Blackie put Regular in and charged her for High-Test.

Whenever Nana filled up at any of the stations, she said the same thing: *Fill it up with High-Test if you please and put it on the charge card.*

Blackie spat every time Nana told him that and wouldn't clean her window or check the dipstick without her asking him to. Uncle Andy said Blackie was in the Klan, that he'd been him in Viet Nam and that his wife had taken him to the cleaners.

Big Blackie. He thinks he's the mayor.

Even though nobody liked Blackie, Nana went to Texaco because she wanted to spread the business. But most of the time we pulled into Buddy Tippin's Sinclair station.

"Well, how yew, Buddy," Nana said and puffed her cheeks out. Buddy always tipped his hat and said,

Well, I'm just fine. How yew, Mizz Matthews?

The first time we filled up at Esso, the man had worn an Esso shirt, but after that, a different man was at the pump every time. Some wore Esso shirts or caps; some didn't. I liked the Esso patch the best with its blue line around the red Esso on white. Both Esso and Mobile were on the other side of town heading up toward the mines. They did more work on cars than Sinclair or Texaco, so they didn't care whether they wore their uniforms or not.

Nana didn't know the man's name at Mobile, but the man wore his smudged red Pegasus hat every time we pulled up. One time the Mobile man wore a Sinclair hat. I looked at the dinosaur then looked at him. He saw me looking and said he had traded hats with Buddy Tippin. He said *I tried to trade with Blackie but Blackie wouldn't do it.* After he had said that, the Mobile man laughed and spat on the ground. Everybody knew *Blackie was the biggest asshole who ever walked the face of the Earth.*

Whenever Duncan whispered *just put it on the charge card* into my ear, I had to pinch my nose as if he had said Cream of Wheat. Another bad one of his was *Here's a little pocket change, a little pocket change, a little pocket change for my favorite.*

Before heading back to the house, Nana took me to either Rexall or the Five-and-Dime. Rexall had air conditioning, chewing gum, and candy in big jars. The Five-and-Dime had peas, pea shooters, sparklers, and models. Nana would usually give me what she called *a little pocket change*. She didn't let me buy pea shooters because she knew the cousins shot peas out of the car window and climbed her dogwoods to shoot peas down at Old May. She knew the pea shooters we bought were extremely accurate.

We'd better not get ourselves a pea shooter today, Rodney. I would just hate to see you or one of the Bass boys get their eye put out by some old pea.

Nana had bought me my BB gun at Couch's hardware when I turned a full nine and didn't say a word about eyes getting put out. I knew it was more likely a cousin or a Bass would accidentally have their eye put out with a BB than a pea.

I knew the real reason. Nana made me cut a switch after I shot a pea out the Olds' back window. The driver in the car blew their horn at Nana after he got hit on the side of his head. Just as soon as we got back to the house, my mother picked out a switch herself and switched me with it while Nana watched. My mother said Nana was furious because she knew the person who had blown his horn. I'd hit him smack on the ear, and he had slapped himself hard thinking it must have been a bee.

My mother sometimes bought the cousins and the Basses pea shooters because she knew it kept us busy. She didn't care if we shot people at stop lights.

Just don't tell me. I don't want to know.

Shooting peas brought me more joy than anything in the world. I liked picking out a new bag of peas at the Five-and-Dime, opening that bag and counting the peas. I didn't waste my peas and took as good care of my peashooter as I did my BB gun. A peashooter lasted a lot longer than a Crystal drive-in straw. Peashooters from the five-and-dime had thicker walls and were cut to just the right length for hitting someone's ear ten feet away.

When my mother drove the cousins into town in either the Comet or the Olds, we'd wait until she pulled up at a red light then duck down in the back seat. One of us raised up and sent a pea into the car that was pulled up beside us. The pea traveled so fast through the air that you couldn't see it but would be able to catch the person smack their neck or jump up in their seat. You ducked as soon as you shot the pea so most of the time you only saw a split second of what happened in the car after that pea hit its target. I couldn't stop laughing whenever I shot my pea no matter what happened. I liked sending a pea into another car more than anything in the world.

I looked forward to going into Knoxville and sitting with the cousins in the back seat and shooting peas at every stop light. We only did that if my mother was driving. My mother pretended she didn't know what was going on. Once I saw my mother look over at a man hitting himself after we had shot a pea and said, Dear God in heaven.

My mother and the cousins couldn't stop laughing after that.

15
THE HOW YEW HOW YEWS, CIVIL DEFENSE, AND PEA SHOOTING

On the ride back to the house, with the windows rolled down, the sound of summer was like a man humming deep in his throat. If I opened my eyes on a hot morning and the sun was already up, the hum was everywhere. It didn't come and go like other sounds and if I didn't listen carefully enough, I'd miss it. If I was able to pick it out, I'd hum along. When we passed fields, the hum became louder, and I tried my best to see where it was all coming from. I wondered if I was the only person in the world listening. The sound of summer that day was so loud, it drowned out nearly everything and I was afraid something else was going to happen, that a Special Report was coming on announcing someone else had been assassinated. I decided to tell Nana about the burlap sack in the tadpole pond and as soon as I did, the sound outside got softer. Before I told Nana anything though, I asked:

"Wasn't it good that the Marines made Clyne a sergeant?"

"Well, I'll say. Your Uncle Andy told me he doubted any branch of the military would take Clyne because he's a fugitive from justice. Your Uncle Andy would be the one to know. He was the youngest person ever to make colonel in the U.S Army."

I told Nana that Munro said Clyne was already at Paris Island and that they were making him a sergeant. Nana spoke in her deep voice:

"I don't think they would make anybody a sergeant. I don't know why Munro would be telling you that."

I decided not to mention the burlap sack to Nana after that, rolled my window up so I didn't have to listen to the hum. I remembered how my head felt watching Clyne's hear-no-evil, and didn't want to think about the see-no-evil for a few minutes, glad he was in the Marines whether they made him a sergeant or not. Something was off about what Munro had told me though. I didn't want to think about what was off.

When we got back to the house, I walked up and down the Florist Shop Road practicing the *how yew how yews,* deciding whether or not to say anything to anybody about what I saw in the tadpole pond. When I thought about something important, whether I was in New York or Tennessee, I paced and practiced the *how yews how yews:*

How yew? Well, how yew? Well, I'm just fine. I added cum up hhrrs, up yonders, the up rrs and I'll says: Well I'll say. I'll Sayyyyy. Well, I'll just say, it's just up yonder. Up rrr, uprrrr up hhrrr up rrrr up rrr uprrr.

I practiced pointing with my chin the way Nana pointed and practiced using my thumb, like Munro. He said, *up rrr,* and pointed with his thumb.

It's up rr.

I also liked to say *Let's head on. Let's head on. You head on. Head on out hair. Head on. Let's head on out.*

Whenever I got home to New York after a summer in

Tennessee, I borrowed one of Dad's tape recorders, recorded the *how yew how yews,* played them back right away and couldn't stop laughing.

When I heard the High Clabbie Clappers auctioneer on the radio in Tennessee, I decided that I didn't want to be a doctor but an auctioneer. Every time we drove past High Clabbie Clappers with the radio on and tuned to the auction channel, I examined the big red barn as carefully as I could. The auctioneer was broadcasting from somewhere inside: *Dibbidibbidibbidibbi hayya dibbidibbidibbi hup dibbidibbidibbi hyonh.*

Being able to speak as fast as the auctioneer at High Clabbie Clappers seemed almost impossible: *DibdibdibdibdibdibHEYdibdibdibittydibbityHEYdibbity.* I didn't think I could look around the auction hall, observe the signals people were sending and keep my *dibitties* going that fast.

Shaw told me that Uncle Andy took him and the twins to High Clabbie Clappers on a Saturday afternoon where they witnessed a man sell his horse for seven hundred dollars by bending his pointing finger. The auctioneer knew what the man meant, kept up his *dibbitydibbities* without missing a beat until he banged the gavel, and the horse was led off.

Shaw said there were one or two auctioneers in the world that could do that and the High Clabbie Clapper's auctioneer was one of them. The other lived in Johnson City.

On that day, I didn't want to think about Clyne or the Marines or the tadpole pond, so I went on to *golly bums* and then the *give us a sup of pops.*

Pat Couch said *Gol-lee Bum* whenever he pitched to us in the Basses back yard field or each time he caught a crawdad. Before we met for baseball every week, Mrs. Bass took us down to crawdad creek. You turned over a flat rock and most of the time there was a crawdad underneath. If it tried to shoot away, you blocked it, scooped creek water into your sandbox bucket and put the crawdad inside. After crawdad creek, we were dropped off at the Jaycees park or taken back to the Bass's house to play. When Pat Couch was on the pitcher's mound, he turned his Braves cap to the side and said *Golleeeee bum.*

Last summer when I played for Citizen's National Bank at the Jaycees Park, I had been standing in the dugout with a cup of Grape Crush when Jesse Goins said:

Roddy, give us a sup uh pop right quick.

Jesse looked down into my cup, asked me for the sup so I gave it to him. The cup was already creased and crumpled, and when I handed it to Jesse, he squeezed the cup a little bit more when he turned it up to take his sup. He handed it straight back though because he was on deck. The cup had started to leak, and I tried to straighten it but couldn't so I swirled what was left of the ice and Grape Crush and poured it all into my mouth.

Let's have us a sup uh pop; give us a sup; give us a sup of your pop right quick. Uh sup uh pop uh sup uh pop uh sup uh pop

The old store down the street from the Jaycees Park sold both Grape and Orange Crush in bottles from the machine under their front window. I liked pushing in my quarter, opening the machine's long door and feeling what it was like for the bottle to give way when I tugged on it.

At the factory in Knoxville, they washed the used bottles, filled them with Crush again and put on the new caps. I especially liked holding a worn one in my hand with its faded lettering but still filled with ice-cold Orange or Grape Crush. We drank our pop in the sun, each of us holding our bottles up after each sip to see where the level sat. You heard your bottle fizz before the swell of katydids drowned the fizzing like being washed over by a wave.

The last things I practiced were Nana's sayings. Nana always picked up the phone at her front hallway desk and said: *Klondike 772. This is Dinah D. Matthews.*

I stood in the kitchen doorway when I could to watch Nana standing by her hallway phone table and speak to the operator.

This is Dinah DEEEE Matthews.

How yew? Well, I'm just fine. . .

Nana sounded as if she was meeting the operator on the church steps. Her *I'll says* went up and down like a yo-yo, depending on what she was telling her.

Well, I'll say. . . I'll say. Well, I'll say.

Duncan came up beside me and imitated Nana right in my ear: *This is Dinah D. Matthews. Dinah Deeeeee Matthews. Dinah D., Dinah D. Matthews, Dinah Deeeeeeeeeeeeeeeeeeeeeeeee Matthews.*

I jerked my head away and couldn't stop laughing.

~

That night Nana served us creamed corn for dinner. She had more cans of creamed corn in her pantry than were stocked on the shelves at Griffith's Department Store. While I sat at the kitchen table, I liked to open the pantry door and examine the cans. If I removed a can, my mother told me to put it back where I found it.

She'll know if any of them are out of place. The same cans of corned beef hash have been sitting on that pantry shelf for twenty years. Some of them have been there since Daddy died. She doesn't throw anything out. Nothing.

Nana's cans were of historical interest. When the Bass Boys visited, I gave them a tour of the pantry and during that tour, explained that some cans were over twenty years old. I reached in all the way to the back and brought out the oldest ones I could find to hold up for them to examine.

This can of Lima Beans is from civil defense, I would say and was careful to point out dents or areas of rust. My mother slid all the civil defense cans against the back wall so Nana couldn't reach them and open them up for our dinner.

Dad had told me to be very careful of Nana's pantry: *Some cans had been there for decades, and more than likely contain botulism. They could be absolutely lethal, and it is conceivable that one might even contract trichinosis from the Spam.*

Trichinosis was Dad's favorite disease, and Spam was Dad's favorite food.

That's all the English had after the war, you see: Spam and sardines.

The old cake that Nana kept in the basement freezer was also part of the Bass boys' tour. I took them down the basement stairs and told them all to lift their legs up like Tennessee Walking Horses because of the snake that lived in the stacks of newspapers. Then I led them past the washer and dryer over to Nana's freezer and pointed through the glass at the old ice cream cake that had been there for fifteen years. The cake had been baked in the shape of a cow but now looked like a monkey. Nana didn't talk about her cow cake, and it was sad to look at but fascinating for those taking the tour.

"How could it be in there for fifteen years?" John Bass always asked. I didn't have an answer. We stood in front of the freezer and examined it carefully through the frosted glass.

When I opened Nana's refrigerator in Tennessee, a plate of meat loaf, a bowl of Jello and a gallon of milk always sat on the middle shelf. In New York, we had the big red tongue on a platter beside either a plate of raw hamburger or raw frankfurters. I never got tired of looking at the big red cow tongue and would sometimes open the refrigerator in the middle of the night, take a pinch of raw hamburger and eat that while examining the tongue.

Nana baked us gingerbread men whenever there came a frost. As soon as the oven door opened, she wrapped them in a paper towel and handed them to us. We ran out into the front yard and I usually ate the legs first, the head last. It was hard to eat the gingerbread man's head. I sometimes left it alone.

Nana brought out a tureen of gravy and a tureen of creamed corn that night. She ladled the creamed corn onto my plate, smacked the mashed potatoes down with her wooden spoon and tapped off the rest. Nana sliced the meatloaf and lifted the slice with her serving spatula, sliding it off onto my plate.

"Let me give you some of this good gravy," Nana said. She ladled gravy over the top of both my meatloaf and mashed potatoes.

I liked to watch Nana mix the mashed potatoes before dinner. She dropped a block of butter into the bowl making a yellow curve. Sometimes I could still see the yellow swirl on my plate. I pushed my fork down into the mashed potatoes and made a lake of gravy. You could change the color of the gravy by twisting in more butter or draw purple lines in by using your beets. I loved twisting beets into my mashed potatoes and watching the purple swirl appear and disappear.

~

At the end of the week, something happened after I shot a pea. On the day it did, Nana had taken all the other cousins to Sheldon's for their shoes. As I had already got mine, I brought my peashooter down to the bank right above Tennessee Avenue and lay flat on my stomach listening to each car *fuff* as it passed. After listening to the first few *fuffs*, I decided it was time to shoot.

After the next *fuff*, I raised and shot. The second I did, the whole car filled the road in front of me, and I could see its windows were rolled all the way down. The car swerved sideways, ran straight through the Basses white fence and into their front yard. I got up and ran as fast as I could as if I were dodging bullets, hiding behind trees until I made it to the house. I ran up the stairs, down the hall, into my room, lay on the bed and didn't want to look out the window. I had never seen anything like that in my entire life, a car driving straight through the Basses fence and into their front yard like *The Green Hornet*. After sitting on my bed remembering over and over how the car looked driving through the Basses fence, I searched everywhere for my peashooter but couldn't find it. My chest felt like it was being squeezed.

I searched the edge of the garden the next morning and looked between every blade of grass around the spot where I had been laying. I remembered getting up and running but couldn't remember whether I had been holding my peashooter. I walked back the way I had run three times and still couldn't find it. I looked on every step of the staircase and under my bed.

I didn't tell a soul about the pea I had fired the moment before the car turned sideways. Clyne had bragged about shooting the boy out of the tree in Bonnet Lake. I wasn't going to brag about shooting my pea at the car even though I could. I would stay the only person on the face of the Earth who had seen the man's car swerve across the road. I didn't know if that swerving had anything to do with my pea.

The next day, Nana was talking on the hallway phone. I was standing in the doorway of the kitchen, listening. After the *how yew how yews,* she said,

"Yes, that's right. Buddy Tippin's wrecker finally was able

to pull it off their fence."

Then, after a minute of listening, she said, "Well, I'll say."

Then she said, "Well."

I didn't know if they were still talking about the car crashing through the Basses fence or not. I hoped she was talking about something else. I hoped that my pea didn't have anything to do with that man and his car. I had puffed air into my peashooter and hadn't seen the pea after that. I hoped my pea wasn't in the man's car; that he would find it and hold it up between two fingers and say,

This is a pea from a peashooter. Who has a peashooter that lives near here?

I imagined all the things the man might have done after getting hit on the side of his head by my pea; like slapping himself or blinking or yanking the wheel.

As this was an emergency, I prayed to God: "Don't let my pea be found."

God already knew I had shot a pea into the road and God already knew what I was worried about; that my pea would be found and that I was going to get caught. God knew I was more worried about getting caught than about the man and his car.

"Dear God, please do not let my pea have anything to do with that man's car."

Nana always asked me at night if I had said my bedtime prayers and I would always tell her, *Yes, Nana.*

My mother told me that bedtime prayers were the chance

to thank everybody I knew. I forgot to pray most of the time, but now and then I did. I thanked Nana if we had gone to the five-and-dime and said, *God Bless my cousins; God bless the Basses; God bless Mom* and *God Bless Dad.* I sometimes said, *God Bless the Three Willoughby Sisters; God Bless Munro;* and *God Bless Old May.*

I prayed whenever I got myself into a mess that I couldn't get out of. I knew God would already know what had happened and knew that I would be praying before I even started or thought about starting. God saw all and knew what part of the man's head my pea had hit, exactly what the man did after it hit him and where both my pea and peashooter both were.

I prayed: "I am sorry that I did not pray before, but I need help, dear God."

The pea was so small; how could it be found? The pea could have bounced on the inside of the car and rolled under the seat. I hoped that was what happened.

I didn't ask anybody about the man in the car but overheard my mother saying the man's head had smashed through his windshield and that he had a wheelchair in his back seat. That's what made it bad. The man couldn't walk to begin with then crashed his car through the Basses fence with his head going through the windshield. Nana told my mother that the man lay there in the front seat then came to and had to do everything by himself after that. He crawled out of the driver's seat and crawled all the way to the Basses front door. Both Mr. and Mrs. Bass were hard of hearing so the man lay there until another car stopped and they called an ambulance to take him to the hospital.

This made it worse.

The man fractured his skull on the windshield, Uncle Gavin had said.

The man was ok it turned out but had to stay in the hospital. No one asked me if I had been in the front yard and I didn't say I had been. I remember firing the pea but couldn't imagine my pea doing that. I felt a little bit angry at the man for letting the tiny little pea crash his car. I didn't tell anybody anything. I didn't want to.

16

OLD MAY SAYS PEASHOOTER, LURCH COMES TO THE BACK DOOR, AND SPEAK NO EVIL

A few days after the pea shooting, I found a dead garter snake in a flower pot on the back porch. I took one of Nana's Ball Jars from the floor of the pantry, filled it with water, dropped the snake in and screwed the lid on tight.

Whatever you put in a Ball jar lasts forever, Nana had told me.

I buried it under one of the dogwoods half way down the driveway, and imagined someone digging up the ball jar in a hundred years, holding it up to the light and being surprised at what they saw. The trees may have all been taken down by then, and everything on the face of the Earth might be different. I hoped not. I did not like thinking about astronauts trapped on an Earth of the future with talking apes living there then seeing the Statue of Liberty buried up to her neck in the sand, knowing there was no way to get back to the good old days.

As soon as I covered the hole with dirt and twigs, Old May limped around the stone posts at the end of the driveway, talking and yelling at the same time, and came jerking up the driveway. I climbed the dogwood tree and lifted my legs up onto a small branch so she wouldn't see them dangling there. Old May stopped right below my tree. She didn't look up but stood there then said,

"Peashooter." Then she sneezed.

I was sure I heard Old May say, "peashooter." I sat still and pushed my back against the trunk of the dogwood. I didn't know why she said that word. I didn't move.

Peashooter was the last word I wanted to hear Old May say. How could Old May know anything about peashooters or be interested in them? I thought about my missing peashooter then about Old May watching everything from the woods.

I couldn't be sure Old May had said *peashooter* and couldn't be sure if she knew I was up in the tree right above her head. She started talking but didn't move from her spot and never once looked up.

"You're going up up up up that hill," she said in a loud deep voice. "Up, up, up that hill." I didn't understand why Old May would be saying that or why she was standing underneath my tree out of all the trees along Nana's drive. Old May started humming. I listened very carefully but couldn't hear her transistor, what my mother told me she hummed along with. All I could hear was the hum of summer. Old May might have been humming along with that, not a transistor radio buried under one of her coats. I imagined my peashooter sitting alongside her transistor, buried under one of her eight layers of coats that she wore all year round.

As I imagined my peashooter stuck down inside one of her layers of coats, Old May started walking again. I felt pressure inside of me like I was a balloon filling up with air. Old May might have been in the woods watching and seen me shoot that pea right before the man's car ran off the road. Old May seemed to know everything I had ever done or hadn't done.

That night Shaw said he saw the old woman in the basement, the same woman he told me he sometimes saw standing down by the gazebo on some nights. I didn't get a good feeling about this old woman. She was someone I didn't want to meet. Shaw made it into a dare to open the basement door and go downstairs with the lights turned off.

There was a mirror on the front of the basement door with a BB hole in the center. Shaw's older brother Rick tried to shoot Shaw with a BB gun when he came running into the house, but the BB missed him and hit the mirror instead. I stood in front of the basement door and looked at the BB hole then opened the door and stood at the top of the basement steps, looking down. I stayed at the top of the steps with the door open and leaned forward, noticing the dryer but couldn't quite see the washing machine. I also couldn't see behind the stairs either where the snake lived, so I waited. When I turned away for a split second, turned back and looked down, there she was. The old woman was standing at the bottom of the stairs, bent but looking up straight at me, her hair white and brittle. I ran down the hallway, swung around the newel and took two stairs at a time, passing by Nana lying asleep in her bed with the light on. My mother was in her room sitting in front of her mirror as the woman was coming up the staircase behind me. I wanted to warn them both, to shout but couldn't open my mouth. I couldn't say anything. I couldn't breathe. The woman from the basement was coming up the steps, and I couldn't move.

The sun was up. My legs were hot, so I pushed the covers

off and turned my head to see if the woman was in my room. She wasn't, but there were too many ghosts now, and some of them were now coming after me in my dreams. I turned my head all the way around and looked at the closet door behind the bed. I looked at the doorknob then at the waves of polyurethane on top of the window chest then at the window handle then at the telephone pole across the driveway. It was Sunday morning and I didn't want to go to Bible School.

Nana gave the Willoughby sisters a ride to church, and Lurch talked the whole way, more than she usually did. As soon as the three of them climbed into the back seat, Lurch turned to the younger one, Stib, and said, "I want you singing the song of innocence this morning, as loud as you can sing."

I looked up into the rearview mirror at Kezia and couldn't help craning my neck to examine her big titties. When I glanced farther up and saw Kezia staring straight at me, I shut one of my eyes and picked at its lid with my finger, pretending something was underneath it. Lurch kept talking the whole time and the more she talked, the more worried I got. She talked louder and louder as if she was preaching from the back seat of Nana's Olds.

"Well, I'll say," Nana said.

Old May had never talked this loud before. I glanced up in the rearview mirror at Lurch. Now it was Lurch who was looking right at me with the yellow bow on top of her head as big as a Christmas wreath.

"And be not deceived, the fornicators will not inherit the kingdom of heaven and the tiger will be coming soon and after he comes and does what he needs to do, I'll be telling the tiger, git back to your hellfar! Git on back to hell, tiger. T-Y-G-E-R, burning bright. Git back on into hellfar."

My mother told me later that the older sister was insane but knew her Bible and took it dead seriously. My mother said felt sorry for the other two Willoughby sisters because the older one bossed the other two around constantly:

"Constantly. She reminds me of Mother. Beats them. That's why Kezia is rebelling, you see. I was that way."

Lurch had spelled tiger wrong. Tiger was spelled T-I-G-E-R, not T-Y-G-E-R.

~

The next day Shaw took the salt shaker off the kitchen table and told us: "Snails can't take salt."

The cousins followed him out of the front door, and we all saw the long trail of slime cutting across the porch. The snail had almost made it to the wall when Shaw shook the salt on it. The snail didn't stop moving but turned sideways. Shaw told us there was a difference between a slug and a snail but wasn't sure what that difference was; the salt affected one of them more than the other. He wasn't sure which one got it worse.

While we were watching the salted snail, Lurch, the oldest Willoughby, came walking up the driveway with Old May limping twenty feet behind her. Lurch carried a walking stick as big as a tree branch, like Moses, taking long and careful steps as if she were walking over stones, fording a river. Nana was already outside and pulling weeds around the holly bush when Lurch reached the front steps, leaned on her stick and said,

"Praise God. I've just been listening to May Vanover outside the Post Office. May Vanover told me that my sister Kezia was being raped on your property by the Presley boy yesterday afternoon, so I asked her to come up here and tell you this herself, Praise God."

Before Old May made it to the porch, I slipped inside the front door and stood stock still, listening.

"Well, I'll say, Jemima." Nana sounded as if she was talking to the operator on the hallway telephone. "Now you just follow me straight into my kitchen."

I ran down the hallway, up the stairs and crouched behind the banister. Nana came in through the front door with Lurch. The smell walked in afterward like a big wet dog.

Clyne was *the Presley boy*. It sounded as if Old May had gotten things mixed up. Clyne had joined the Marines. She couldn't have seen him the day before. I walked down the hallway and sat on the edge of my bed.

Duncan came upstairs later: "Oh God, Roddoh. Guess who came up to the back door. Guess!"

I already knew who had come up to the back door but asked him "Who?"

"Old May! Oh my GOD, Roddoh, Lurch was standing in the middle of the kitchen telling Nana that Kezia

Willoughby had been bent over the gazebo bench and Clyne had been raping her from behind yesterday morning. Old May was standing behind the screen door saying, 'raping her from behind' and told Nana she'd been standing in the woods watching it!"

Duncan was laughing but I couldn't laugh and couldn't breathe. Munro told us all that Clyne had joined the Marines.

"Old May was watching it," Duncan repeated.

After Duncan had told me that, Shaw stuck his head in my room and said, "Let's all check the snail." I didn't want to go outside but followed them out anyway. The snail was foaming yellow. I bent over and stayed still. I didn't want to look at the snail.

Duncan told Shaw, "Old May came up to the screen door and told Nana about Clyne busting Lurch's sister. Nana handed them both a glass of lemonade! O NA NAW!" Duncan imitated Nana. "'Here's some of this good lemonade.'"

"Old May told Nana 'Someone may be fixin' to kill that Presley boy.' Nana said she would call the sheriff from the hall phone, but Lurch told her, 'No, Praise God! He's just about useless.'" Duncan imitated Old May's deep voice. "'That Sheriff won't be doin' a goddamn thing. The goddamn Sheriff knows all about the Presley boy shooting up in Bonnet Lake and didn't do a goddamn thing.'"

After Lurch and Old May had left, the cousins went back into the kitchen table, and Nana brought out the Debbie Cakes. My mother, Adair and Uncle Andy were already drinking ice tea.

"Well, I guess Clyne didn't join the Marines."

"Aw hell, Munro told me he'd given him a ride out of town and told him to stay away. The Marines were no more going to take Clyne than they would John Dillinger."

"Old May was telling mother after Jemima left that Kezia looked like she was laughing when they were having sex. Of course, she was laughing. But Old May didn't tell Jemima Willoughby that, you see. She wants to stir up trouble. 'Wahl I deent tell har THAT.' My mother imitated Old May's deep voice. Everybody laughed.

Uncle Andy said, "Old May watching them have sex, Gawd Almighty. Perseus told me he screwed Kezia on his table up at the Florist Shop last year."

My mother said, "No, I don't think the big one understands what's going on. I feel sorry for all three of them. Poor old things."

I went back out with Duncan to see the snail again, which had turned into a puddle. We sat back down on the steps.

"Oh my God! Lurch, YOU RANG?" Duncan said. "Roddoh, can you believe Lurch telling Ole Na Naw, 'He was raping my sister on your property.' Can you imagine Lurch saying that?"

I still couldn't breathe and couldn't say anything, feeling like I was asleep in the middle of my nightmare. Bodies were sunk at the bottom of the tadpole pond, Clyne was back, and I was accessory to the crime. Duncan imitated Old May's deep voice:

"We don't want the goddamn Sheriff."

After that, I told my mother I was sick. She told me I looked white as a ghost and brought bowls of pea soup up to the room. My mother had Uncle Gavin check me and he said it must be a virus. I couldn't eat my dinner and went to bed early while the cousins were outside playing flashlight tag. The bugs knocked against the streetlight again and again. The burlap bag was under the water in the tadpole pond with the red haired boy wedged underneath it.

Nana walked down the hallway and fell back into my chair by my mother's door.

"Mercy," was always the first thing she said after falling back. "Rindy Anne, I want you to make sure they don't bury me alive."

I was too tired and sick to find my yellow pad and write down what Nana had just said but did find it very interesting.

"Mother, you know that's not going to happen. How would you even think that was going to happen?"

"Mercy, if I was to wake up in a coffin, so helpless like that, in the dark and not being able to catch my breath. Lawsie Mercy! Scratching and knocking and calling out. Law!"

My mother had already told me up in New York that Nana's one fear was being buried alive.

She isn't afraid of anything else.

I remembered Dad saying, *Very interesting* when my mother said Nana was afraid of being buried alive.

~

On Saturday morning, I sat in Nana's room watching Yosemite Sam look at each mouthwatering coconut dish he had fixed himself for dinner while he was living on a deserted island:

"Tossed coconut salad, fresh coconut milk, New England boiled coconut. . ." He stopped talking and yelled: "I hate coconuts!"

At the same time, my mother yelled up the stairs:

"BRODIE'S HERE! COME DOWN AND JUST LOOK AT WHAT HE BROUGHT YOU!"

I didn't expect to come into the kitchen and see the big wooden box sitting on the red-checked tablecloth. When my mother told me Brodie was bringing over a real skull, I was more excited than I had ever been in my life but when it finally arrived in a wooden box with four locks, I wasn't so sure what to think. It looked like a real skull with little pieces of tape stuck to it. Brodie took a full minute to open all the locks and lift the skull out.

Brodie asked Nana not to breathe a word to the other cousins that the skull was coming since too many people would want to touch it. My mother had told Brodie that I wanted to be a doctor, so he made the special trip with his skull. I wanted to be an auctioneer, not a doctor.

Brodie's skull turned out to be a real skull, not a toy. I

could only look at it, not play with it. Brodie borrowed the skull from the University of Tennessee. It wasn't his to keep. I wasn't sure how to play with the skull. Before Brodie showed up, I imagined looping my fingers through the skull's eye sockets and carrying it up and down the driveway, but after seeing it come out of the box, I didn't want to touch it.

Brodie explained the different parts of the skull then put it back in its box, latched the four locks and we went out into the driveway. He showed me how to tie the string to my yo-yo, throw it straight out, loop it back over my hand, drop it down to the ground and jerk it back up. I liked feeling my yo-yo zooming out, spinning around, coming back into my hand while whizzing and whirring, like Odd Job's hat. All the cousins had gone to see Goldfinger in Knoxville. Odd Job and his hat were the one thing I remembered. Odd Job could throw his hat, knock someone's head off, and watch the hat return to his hand.

My yo-yo had a red side and a blue side. You had to wind the string gently, or it would hang up as soon as it hit bottom on the first throw. If the yo-yo stayed down, you had to rewind it.

By the time Brodie had left with his skull, all the cousins had gone down to the cemetery to look at my grandfather's gravesite. Munro's truck wasn't in the driveway and I hadn't heard any crunching of gravel. All I heard were the sounds of summer rising and falling out the kitchen screen door so I came outside holding my new P51 above my head and ran across the Florist Shop Road. I had glued the model the night before and that morning added the decal with the round star and two blue stripes on both wings. I had been watching how the decals looked with the plane in the air and ran half way down the garden steps before I saw the two boys inside the gazebo.

Clyne was standing in front of another boy who wore a Braves shirt. Clyne looked up and saw me, turned and hit the boy in his nose. Blood dripped onto his Braves shirt, running as fast as a faucet. The boy started to cough and didn't stop. Clyne held the boy by his arm because the boy was trying to get away. Clyne called up to me.

"You're my Supreme Court Witness. I caught this one tattling on my whereabouts, so I've sentenced him to speak-no-evil. Hand us that bottle by my feet!"

Clyne nodded toward the bottle of lye resting on the gazebo seat. Nana kept the can of lye in her basement between the washer and dryer. I didn't know why Clyne had asked me to get it as he was standing right beside the can.

I ran back up the garden steps, stopped and looked back. Clyne hit the boy again and again with his balled-up fist and the boy went down on one knee. I crossed the florist shop road and went down on one knee as well. I looked at the ground then looked back down into the garden. Clyne had dragged the boy down the gazebo steps holding the bottle in his other hand then yelled, "Hold yourself still!"

I was going to vomit because Clyne had the boy by the hair and I could see the boy's eyes looking at me.

Clyne pulled the boys head back, reached down and stuck the bottle into his mouth like he was pouring laundry detergent into the top of Nana's washing machine.

I needed to bend over and had to wait until the vomit

came up while Clyne was dragging the boy into the cat grass where Snow White and the black snake lived. The boy was kicking as I was vomiting. Clyne saw me sitting down on the Florist Shop Road vomiting and yelled up:

"I'll tell them YEW poured it!"

Clyne was lying. I didn't pour the lye. While I was running back into the house, with vomit still hosing out of my mouth, I had to turn my head to spray it onto Nana's rhododendrons behind the back porch before I ran into the kitchen. I ran up the stairs, down the hallway and walked back and forth in my room from door to window. I had to do something and finally saw the yellow pencil sitting on the table beside my bed, picked it up, carried it over to the window, put my hand flat on the sill, raised the pencil up and came down as hard as I could. I didn't move my hand and fell on the floor after looking at the pencil sticking out the other side. The summer buzzing was coming and going. I couldn't pull the pencil out and didn't want to move my hand but got up, walked across the hallway and showed my mother.

My mother screamed for Uncle Gavin, and before I knew what he was going to do, he pulled the pencil out and was looking at my hand. Nothing had broken off inside, so he took me to the bathroom sink and washed my hand with soap and water. He made me move my fingers back and forth and asked me to push and pull one finger at a time. He gave me antibiotic tablets and wrapped my hand.

"Ohh Roddoh." Uncle Gavin laughed. I hadn't told, but I did something. I didn't want to see the boy with Clyne like I had seen or see what Clyne had done. I didn't want to see the boy moving like he had been moving, and the pouring

and the boy trying to get away from Clyne. I had seen
enough and didn't want to see any more.

17
YOU WHORE, SHARKS IN THE WATER, AND SNAKE HANDLING

After finishing my Cream of Wheat the next morning, I walked straight out the back door, down the garden steps and pushed my way through the pile of sticks in front of the tadpole pond. When I felt the touch on my forehead, I stopped. The long spindle of the spider's web stretched from the oak behind the pond all the way over to the rhododendron beside me. When I moved, the web shook, and its drops twinkled. With one finger, I pulled the thread off my hair, the web snapped and shot away like a rubber band. The top half bobbed up and down and it was then I saw the dead granddaddy longlegs laying on a little hill of burlap that stuck up out of the water. I pushed my way back out, relieved. Nothing new had been added to the tadpole pond since the last time I looked. As the web had been so big, the spider would have had to start making it before I even saw Clyne and the boy with the Braves shirt. I stood on the gazebo steps: The ground had been raked again, but the cat grass wasn't even bent in the place where the boy had been dragged. I hoped more than anything in the world the boy with the Braves shirt had gotten away.

The summer buzz swelled up, died down and swelled up, trying to tell me something over and over that I couldn't understand. Shaw said grasshoppers rubbing their legs together made that sound, and that they did it all at the same time by some kind of secret signal. I always turned my head in different directions, looking through the woods but could never find the place where it all came from.

A little while later, we all piled in the Olds, took a drive over to the Crystal and asked them to make ten cheeseburgers to go. Coming back, the buzzing was louder on the Loop with the window rolled down than it had ever been. The buzzing was all I heard.

That night the woods croaked as if an old witch was sitting down in the gazebo, laughing into her microphone:

Heh heh heh heh   Heh heh heh heh   Heh heh heh heh.

I stood at the top of the stairs and cranked the window farther open. There was silence after each laugh and the quiet in between was as loud as the laugh itself. I had heard the witch laughing before but never with silence in between that loud. If you happened to take the Loop at night with the windows rolled down, all you heard was laughing.

Heh heh heh heh. . . .HEH HEH HEH HEH.

The pitch black in Nana's garden filled every space and even with light shining down on it from my mother's upstairs window, no light ever came back. I never went down into the garden at night and never brought up going into the garden at night with the Daredevils Club because, even though it was a good idea for a dare, I didn't want Shaw making it into one.

I dropped myself down into the chair by the door of my mother's room because I had been thinking about telling her what I saw Clyne do to the boy with the Braves shirt. I looked at the paperback book sitting on her mirror table: *Valley of The Dolls.* My mother had paperback books on her makeup table and her bed. She read a paperback almost every day.

I eat up a good book.

I was nearly finished with my *Arabian Nights*. On its cover was a picture of the King in his turban lying down on the bed with Scheherazade sitting on the floor in front of him, telling him a story to keep him occupied. On the cover of my mother's *Valley of the Dolls* were big bottle of medicine and a man standing in a doorway. He looked like I might have looked if I had done something and my mother had made me go out in the garden to cut a switch. I got up and opened the other paperback sitting on my mother's bedside table. The lady on its cover was pulling up her stockings with a man standing behind a screen door looking at her. The man wasn't wearing a shirt. I turned to page twenty-three. A man said:

"You whore!"

"Yes, I'm a whore," Sarah, the woman in the book, said.

Adair had mentioned in the den that Perseus had a *whore*.

I had already asked Munro what a whore was. He told me I was *going to hell* if I said that word out loud. I looked at the woman's stockings on the cover of the book then looked at the man without a shirt.

I didn't tell my mother about Clyne. As I sat, I figured out he had to have come inside Nana's house to get her bottle of lye out of the basement; and if he could do that, he could come back in and gouge our eyes out. I was still his Supreme Court Witness, accessory to his crime and had my own crimes as well to worry about.

After Sunday school that week, I had a fight with my mother because she wanted me to spend the rest of the afternoon outside with the cousins. I couldn't because Clyne was out there, so I yelled at her and she yelled back at me to cut my own switch. I went out into the front yard and cut a big branch off a rhododendron and brought it back up to the porch. My mother took the switch, but as soon as she did, I grabbed it back and yelled:

"No, you whore!"

I had never seen my mother so mad. I dropped the switch and ran inside. She came running in after me, so I ran upstairs and into my room and slammed the door. As I would rather put off my switching until later, I pushed myself against the door while my mother banged and shoved from the other side.

I yelled through the door: "You WHORE!" I yelled whore three more times: "Whore whore WHORE!"

I liked the sound of just whore without the "you." "Whore" sounded better than "you whore."

"WHORE!" I yelled.

"What did you call me? What did you call me? NEVER CALL ME A WHORE AGAIN!"

I didn't know what whore was, and she was getting even angrier, so I shouted it louder, "WHORE WHORE WHORE!" I was surprised how angry it made her. She hit the door with the flat of her hand.

It wasn't my fault.

When I came out of my room, my mother had calmed down but still made me cut another switch. If she had been very angry, she would have picked up the first thing she saw and spanked me with it, so I knew the right thing to do had been to wait. When I went into the front yard to find a bush for my switch, I saw the piles of sawdust where Munro had been cutting his two by fours out by the cousin's new treehouse. Big black ants were climbing over the sawdust piles as well as on the bark of the trees. I looked down and saw the big black ants crawling through the grass as well. Those were harder to see, and I wouldn't have known to look for them there if I hadn't first noticed them in the sawdust. I watched the big black ants on the sawdust pile for a little while before I cut my switch and brought it to my mother.

After getting switched, I sat on the stairs and watched Nana go into the kitchen and close the door behind her. She never closed the kitchen door. I put my head against the door and heard her tell my mother that they found a boy in the woods. After that, I only heard murmuring. When I heard footsteps, I climbed to the top of the stairs and listened to Nana make a phone call in the downstairs hallway.

"Klondike 772. This is Dinah D. Matthews."

"Why yes. How yew? Well, I'm just fine. . .Well, I'll say. The service will be Saturday then. Yes, I heard it was. . . Yes. I heard it was. Well, I'll say. I'll say."

Nana's "I'll says" were very quiet that day. I knew something happened to the boy. I went into the bathroom, unwrapped the bandage and looked at the hole in my hand. I put my hand under the sink and ran the water over the hole and jerked it back. I turned the water on full and put my hand under the water and stood it.

~

That night the man from the closet turned up a second time. He had never showed up twice in one summer. I turned my head and there he was, not smiling, not looking angry, but staring up at the ceiling like he usually did. He lay on the window side of my bed wearing his clothes and shoes just like the last time, holding his arms straight down by his side like the postcard Dad had sent me of the guard standing in front of Buckingham Palace. I turned away like I usually did, but when I turned back, he began twisting his head very slowly around in my direction and ended up looking straight at me, not moving a muscle. I didn't move a muscle either. My head stayed turned to the side just like his. He blinked. I had never seen the ghost blink before. He looked to be on the verge of saying something but didn't. He looked like he had done a lot of work that day and was worn out.

I didn't recite the Lord's Prayer like I did in the middle of a nightmare when Evil was standing close but just lay there watching him. I wasn't sure how to feel about the Man from the Closet showing up a second time. I stared at him a little while longer then got out of bed. This time, the ghost followed me with his eyes as if he still had something to say. I walked out of the bedroom door but didn't feel a hand on my shoulder or hear rustling as if he was raising an ax above his head. I peed then went back to my room. The ghost was gone. This time, I opened the closet door and pulled the string that traveled over three hooks and attached itself to a bulb against the cedar wall. I looked carefully at all the boxes in the closet and at the fishing equipment piled in the back. Nothing looked different than the last time I had examined the inside of the closet so I stepped out and turned.

A large brush looked to have wiped orange day-glo along the floor out my mother's door, across the hall and over the foot of my bed. I lay back down and watched the bugs zig-zag around the streetlamp while the woods rose and fell.

I swam and felt that the shark nearby. I couldn't see it under the surface, although was certain the shark knew of my whereabouts. Because it remained out of sight and underneath, I stepped out onto the beach, too scared to swim. As soon as I was no longer afraid, I waded back in. I don't know why I would do this as the shark was still swimming nearby, but I did. Something pushed me, I felt my chest tighten and got out for a second time to examine the surface of the ocean and the all gray sky. When I was no longer afraid, I returned to the ocean, this time thin wooden planking had been laid down over the water, safer than swimming but not much safer: It wobbled. I could still see nothing below the surface and continued to walk over the boards, following their travel inside a large pavilion containing a deep tank fed by the same ocean. There, I looked down past the wood into the crystal clear water, dark blue, and filled with hundreds of sharks, not small ones but big ones. I knew they had been there all along, both inside and out. I jerked my eyes open and turned over in bed to see the shining polyurethane and the morning dew on my window sill.

My mother and I liked to take the Asbury Park bus out of Port Authority and eat clam chowder at the Howard Johnson's and drink fresh-squeezed orange juice at the boardwalk stand. I woke up thinking about one day in particular. The sky had turned dark gray, and it began sprinkling. We had walked toward the old pavilion and stopped before entering because something was happening in the ocean. We stood at the railing, both of us examining the waves.

The old pavilion had been scheduled to be torn down. They kept the doors open to let the people pass through to the next stretch of boardwalk leading to a slightly newer pavilion that had ski ball, prizes in glass cases, cotton candy, and fudge. The restaurant was the only business left open in the old one but its wooden housing leaned so far out over the water on slanted pilings that people were afraid to eat there. Plywood boards were nailed over some windows the ocean had broken.

My mother told me: *Don't look.*

It was too late. I already had. The sky had been glued behind the ocean like black construction paper with the clouds cut out and white paper pasted behind the black. The water was not blue or green but white and gray, rising straight to the top of the old pavilion and crashing down, over and over. As the ocean rose, the sharks hung inside each wave, behind a thin curtain. No one else besides my mother and I had seen the sharks. The ocean hadn't been a dream. I would have only wanted to see sharks inside waves like that in my nightmares. I could wake up from a nightmare. The sharks that day had been real, all of them near the shore. Sharks were always under the water.

~

That Sunday afternoon, we all piled in the Olds and drove out to the tent revival. Munro's church handled snakes every Sunday afternoon, and he told Nana that we could all come that particular Sunday, stay in the car and watch. Munro was a snake handling Deacon for the Mountain Church of God with Signs Following.

This is odd they're letting outsiders watch. They're usually very private although what I heard was this minister was trying to get his own TV show in Knoxville and had been letting people in to film him during handling. He combs his hair back, you see.

I sat in the back seat with Cameron, Lillian, and Duncan. Shaw was with the Twins, Adair and Uncle Andy in the other car.

"They're handling outside today," Nana said. "This is so nice of Munro to invite us. Be sure and thank him."

A big white tent was set up on a hill on a small road past the drive-in, with people waving us into their parking spot on the grass. Snake handling was the most exciting thing I ever wanted to see in my life, so when we pulled up in the Olds and waited for the tent flap to open, I almost couldn't stand it and had nearly forgotten about Clyne. People came out one by one then finally a man in a white shirt.

215

Nana said, "Rodney, Cameron, Lillian: Here comes the preacher."

I couldn't understand the preacher. He used a microphone and spoke as fast as the auctioneer at High Clabbie Clappers. "Holy Ghost huunna hunna YAH! holy ghost an uh hunna hunna hunna HAH   hunna hunna holy ghostuh!

"Law mother, that's Arnold Clinton. I knew him from school. Look at him. Jo Ann Bass said they call him the Silver Fox."

Nana pointed a bent finger toward the Reverend Arnold Clinton. His white hair was pulled up and combed straight back, shining in the sun.

"He uses Vaseline," my mother said.

Nana turned and looked at us in the back seat and puffed her cheeks out. The Reverend kept yelling and talking. We kept our windows rolled up and the car doors locked. Nana turned around and said: "The snakes are coming soon."

Reverend Clinton jolted, and his congregation clapped. One woman danced up and down then bounced against one of the men, who caught her. She put her hands on the man and flinched. There was an old woman then a younger woman who also began flinching, then another man started jumping. People held up their hands.

"Oh, Jesus Hubbity Hubbity uh. Oh, Jesus hubbity hubbity hubbbity uh."

The Reverend Arnold Clinton kept saying words over and over, and I couldn't understand them, but every few seconds he added "uh!"

The congregation came outside the tent and stood in front of the cars. Their arms came up while they sang hymns. The car was getting hot, but Nana didn't want us to roll down the windows. The snakes hadn't come out yet, and the singing was as boring as it was in our church.

Finally, Nana said, "Here come the snakes!"

Four old men came out of the tent flap holding up snakes. I didn't see where they got their snakes, but suddenly there was snake handling all around the cars.

"Just Look at those old Pentecostals," Nana said. "Oh, and Rindy, there's Munro! LAWSIE! Rodney, lookie there. Munro is holding a big buck Timber Rattler!"

Munro was standing right in front of the Olds, holding up a copperhead! He had come right up to the front of the Olds and stood there, holding his Timber Rattler up.

"Rodney, look over here, right quick. That's a Timber Rattler Munro's holding. I want you to see. Rindy, roll down your window, I'm going to wave Munro over."

"Mother, NO!" my mother said. Munro was jerking. I didn't want Munro waved over either.

"Oh he's too much," my mother said. "I wish Dad was here. Freddy would love this. Dear GOD, look at him!"

The windows were rolled up, and Nana rustled a Debbie cake wrapper. I looked out at Munro flinching, holding up his rattler.

"Law, MOTHER," my mother said.

"Mmm mm," Nana said. "Just look at that big buck Timber Rattler!"

Old people walked around the cars with bundles of copperheads and rattlers in their hands. The Silver Fox was talking faster than he had before, *hubbity hubbity hubbity HA*. This time, he yelled out *HA* after each bunch of words instead of *uh*. The *HA* was louder than the *uh*. From the back seat, I couldn't make out any of his other words, just the *HA*.

18
YABLONSKI, ARABIAN NIGHTS, AND SOCKS TO THE RESCUE

When we got back from the revival, Nana had gone upstairs. A Special Report had come on, but she only called my mother in to watch, closing the bedroom door behind her. I stood outside and listened to the television announcer as well as to Nana's *mm mmming*. The Special Report was about Yablonski. I had already seen many Special Reports about Yablonski up in New York and was tired of hearing about him. Yablonski had been killed after Christmas. My mother had stood in front of the TV that entire Special Report and shook her head then called everybody in the family one by one. They had shown pictures of the Yablonski house with police waiting outside. They showed the house for an hour straight but nothing else. Yablonksi was United Mine Workers.

My mother said, *Yablonski was known to be a good man.*

When the new Yablonski Special Report came on Nana's TV, it must have shown something that caused Nana to say: "Lawsie Mercy, Rindy Anne!""

I stayed still, tried not to breathe hard, and listened. The police had caught somebody.

"LAW, Rindy Anne!"

"Mm MM," my mother said.

After the door finally opened, Nana said, "Well" and I followed her and my mother downstairs and into her kitchen.

"Oh Rodney, how about I slice you a nice big piece of this good coconut cake and pour you a good glass of whole milk."

My mother said, "They already knew it was that Tony Boyle. Why drag it on and on. That Tony Boyle is too much, isn't he? Mean. My God."

I knew from listening to the Yablonski Special Reports that Tony Boyle was also United Mine Workers and had something to do with it. My mother said Tony Boyle had arranged to kill Yablonski even though they were both United Mine Workers.

"Tony Boyle." I said his name: "Tony Boyle, Tony Boyle."

Later that afternoon, Old May came to the back door to deliver her Sunday Editions of the Press and Tribune then stood outside the screen talking to my mother

I had been eating a Debbie Cake at the kitchen table. When she knocked, I didn't have time to move but could only see the half of her face with the one eye pointing out to the side. When she leaned back, I took my Debbie cake, snuck out into the hallway, and stood there nibbling.

My mother spoke to Old May about Yablonski and Tony Boyle and somebody else I couldn't hear the name of, telling her she had watched the Special Report on television. Old May said television this and television that, and I didn't understand what she was saying in between, but my mother seemed to. My mother spoke to Old May in a whisper. After she did that, Old May raised her voice and yelled out in a crystal-clear voice:

"I know that man and he's no better than a stinking nigger. He killed them all, and he's going to goddamn Tennessee death row. I'd like to be up thar when he hangs to spit on his goddamn dead body. And I'll tell you what. I'd like to spit on that goddamn Tony Boyle's goddamn dead body before he goes down to hell to burn."

After that, Old May started talking to my mother about her change purse. Her voice got louder and louder and louder, her words coming faster and faster *wup wup wup wup WUP*.

Aunt Adair stood beside me and whispered, "Oh Rodney, I think she's telling Rindy that she saw something else happen. I think the poor old thing showed up here trying to protect us."

I tried to listen as carefully as I could to what Old May was saying.

"Jemima Willoughby uprr sid sayn haym born shay brung thayt midwif upere and thayt midwif ran clean away soons that boy camesout thuh groun where hayz mohthers lay up thar blaydin right up thar b'yurn Rex Mine, known thayut bay true."

"Now she's saying Jemima Willoughby told her that Clyne was born on the ground or out of the ground up by Rex Mine. It sounds like she's afraid of Clyne."

Aunt Adair was translating what Old May was saying as if I was a delegate in the United Nations from a different county and had headphones on.

Uncle Gavin had taken both Duncan and I up to Rex Mine to fly Junebugs. Right outside the mine's boarded up entrance was the best spot for catching them. Uncle Gavin taught us how to tie a string around a Junebug's leg and fly it over our heads. Sassafras grew in the woods around the mine shaft as well. Uncle Gavin had dug up a root and cut off a piece for both of us to chew. I wanted more than anything in the world to go back up to Rex Mine, fly Junebugs and dig for sassafras.

When Old May left, my mother came out of the kitchen.

"Poor old thing. They're all so superstitious and take their Bible so literally. I grew up with all that, you see."

Whenever my mother said she grew up with that, she's always added a *you see*.

Adair said, "It sounds like that poor woman may have seen something, Rindy."

My mother said, "Adair, I think you're absolutely right! She MUST have seen something."

~

I finished *Arabian Nights* and brought the book with me when we went back out to the barn with Duncan. With the writing that covered the length of his arm, Socks was the only person I could think of in Tennessee who might be interested in reading it.

Socks had been sitting on a stump behind a brown

Tennessee Walker, the horse's leg resting on top of his knee as he was prying off its shoe. The horse stood still while Socks showed Duncan and me his puller, his rasp, and his hammer. Socks kept the puller and the rasp in his overall loops.

After Socks had explained the three tools, I handed him the book. He held it still for a moment then placed it down beside his foot and finished prying off the rest of the shoe. The horse's penis came down like a hose and he peed straight down into the dirt. The tinkle made a river that flowed straight toward *Arabian Nights*. Without looking down, Socks picked up *Arabian Nights* and laid it on the other side of the stump just as the horse's pee passed by Socks' boot, right in the nick of time. *Arabian Nights* was safe.

I tried to get a better look at Socks' arm, but he was moving it around too much. I wanted to read the words on Socks' arm and understand what those words meant more than anything in the world. I wanted to know why he had taken the trouble to have those words written down the entire length of his arm. Duncan had told me that the words don't make sense to anybody.

After we had got back from the barn, another Special Report came on, this one about the Sharon Tate murder and the Charles Manson Family trial. There had already been a lot of Sharon Tate Special Reports that year. After the first, my mother had called Dad in New York, and they had talked for a long time about Roman Polanski, the husband of Sharon Tate. I had heard so many Special Reports that I wondered if Yablonski knew Polanski and even though the Yablonski murder wasn't the same murder, with one Special Report coming on after another after another, I thought it might be best if Yablonski and Tony Boyle, Sharon Tate and Roman Polanski and Charles Manson should all be together in the same Special Report to cover it all at once. I got so used to Special Reports that if one hadn't come on for a few weeks, I started worrying about when one would, and if the program I watched was going to be interrupted with news of the next person to be assassinated. I began to wish that the next assassination would just happen to get it over with and have the Special Report so we could all find out who was the next one to get it. Waiting for the next Special Report was worse than waiting for the next episode of *The Green Hornet.*

~

I went out to play in the sandbox the next day because The Tennessee State Trooper parked at the end of Nana's driveway had been keeping a look out over Tennessee Avenue. Aunt Adair said:

This was one of the biggest manhunts we have ever seen.

As soon as I sat down in the sandbox with my Messerschmitt, Clyne stepped out of the woods smoking a cigarette.

"Kezia said you were staring at her titties in your granny's car and I'm thinking what she's not saying is that you raped her after your church service because I was waiting for her and she didn't come to me like she was supposed to. You raped the woman I was taking for my wife, and I know you weren't the only one who's raped her. I heard things about that bitch that don't concern you, and went ahead and took full care of it just like I'm going right down my list and just now came to your name. You'll suffer a see no evil, and you knew that you would before you even looked at her."

"Nana was in the car," I told Clyne and moved toward him one step. Clyne needed to know that everybody was in the car when I looked and that I couldn't have raped her.

"I don't have hairs."

I didn't know what to say to Clyne and didn't know why he would even think that. Nana, my mother, and the two other Willoughby sisters had all been in the Olds at the same time. I didn't try to rape Kezia

"I don't have hairs," I told Clyne again. "I came home in the Olds after Bible School."

I didn't know what to say to Clyne, but Clyne grabbed me from behind like a lizard and yanked my hair back then took the cigarette out of his mouth and held it in front of my eye. My legs dropped straight down then started kicking up in the air. Clyne pulled my hair back and said,

"Hold still."

Clyne pulled my left lid down with the hand he had wrapped around my face, and I watched an ash drop off the tip of the cigarette leaving behind a bright red glow.

When Clyne let go of my hair, I fell back onto the slide and hit the back of my head against its edge. I reached up, pressed on the spot that hurt and saw Socks standing by the swing set in his overalls. He moved quicker than I have ever seen him move and jerked Clyne by his neck over to the swing set, pushed his head down on the seat, yanked his shoe puller from the loop of his overalls and pulled Clyne's ear off like I had seen him pull off a horse's shoe. He scraped the puller on his heel and the ear fell off. I was looking straight at Socks' shoes and couldn't turn my head. Neither shoe had laces. Clyne didn't make a sound but held his hand over the hole where the ear had been. As soon as the ear came off, red blood sprayed over Clyne's clothes and blood came out from behind his fingers.

Clyne turned and tried to hit Socks with his other hand, but Socks didn't care and said *pup pup* pup then jerked forward on top of Clyne like I had seen an alligator do in the show at Gatorland in Florida when it had moved to get his fresh chicken. Socks grabbed Clyne by the neck and put Clyne's hand against his knee like a horse's hoof, took his puller out again and jerked off Clyne's finger, the one with a ring on it. Clyne moaned like a cow while Socks scraped the finger off with the heel of his shoe. The finger fell right next to Clyne's ear under one of the swings. The ring had flown off and made a *DANG* when it landed on the slide. Socks picked up Clyne's ring, shined it against his pants, slid it onto one of his own fingers, held it up and cocked his head. Clyne pressed his gushing hand against his shirt, holding the hole on the side of his head with the other one. Clyne didn't make a sound but opened his mouth wider and wider, rocking back and forth.

"Give it here." Socks grabbed hold of Clyne's arm like it was a horse's leg and braced his wrist against his knee, took the rasp out of his belt loop and started rasping the bone sticking out of Clyne's hand. Clyne went down on one knee, and I had to go down on one knee too.

I looked at the ground but listened to the sound of rasping. Socks rasped Clyne's finger then took his puller and yanked off the little piece of bone that was left sticking out and flicked it into the woods. I had to lay my head down on the bottom of the slide and watch the wall of the sandbox. Socks let Clyne go, spit on the ground and slid his tools back through his belt loops. Clyne's hand looked better after the rasping, but he ran off into the woods holding his ear and pressing his hand against his shirt. He ran in the same direction that he had dragged the red-haired boy.

Socks bent down and picked up Clyne's ear and finger then threw them side arm into the woods. The ear and the finger slapped against the leaves *tat tat tat*. Socks turned around and spoke to me as clearly as I had ever heard him speak:

"If he comes again, don't say one word to that son bitch. Let him go his way. It's already done. If it weren't, he'd be my business."

After that, Socks headed straight into the woods toward the Florist Shop. I didn't know if Socks knew Perseus. Socks wasn't moving fast and pushed the branches over to one side so they wouldn't spring back and hit him in the face.

19

BARN WOMAN, GINGER ROSE, TROUBLE WITH OLD MAY, AND MICKEY MANTLE

The Friday night after Clyne's rasping, Duncan told me we were picking up Socks in the Comet by the softball field behind the Baptist Church. He was going to buy us all Tall Boys at the Top Hat drive-through. I never had a Tall Boy. Duncan told me not to say a word to my mother about it so I mentioned we were just going for cheeseburgers at the Crystal before seeing the Batman Movie at the Chippewa Theater. As soon as we got into the Comet, Duncan told me that we were also going to be looking for a *nice big hot plate of pussy*. That worried me. I still didn't have hairs.

When Socks climbed into the Comet, he was carrying my *Arabian Nights*, using an Oakleaf for a bookmark. I never said anything to anybody about Socks' rasping because Socks knew something I didn't and hadn't seemed worried about any of it.

"Tall Boys hubba jubba, goddamn Quart," Socks said after he closed the door.

Duncan drove the Comet up to the Top Hat package store window, Socks leaned his head out and ordered six Tall Boys and two Quarts. Socks opened my first Tall Boy and it made a sound: *SCLORCH*. Socks' Quart made a *SSSSS* when he twisted its cap. He put one finger against his lips, bent forward and spoke so Duncan couldn't hear him:

"What people say is usually a whole lot of bullshit." He spoke louder: "Goddamn King of Beers hubba jubba."

I looked at Socks, thought I had to say something, so I said: "That Tall Boy is the king of beers."

Socks answered right away. "No sir, hubba jubba goddamn Tall Boy king of beer? No sir, goddamn Quart."

Both Duncan and Socks laughed. Socks asked, "Goddamn Tall Boy King of Beer?"

"Oh my God," said Duncan. "Socks loves that you said that. Listen to him."

Socks repeated, "Goddamn Tall Boy, King of Beer, goddamn Quart."

"Guess what, Roddoh," Duncan said, "Ginger Rose wants to go riding with us."

We had the Tall Boys and the Quarts in the car, and I went on sipping mine. The first time I had Tall Boy in my mouth, I didn't want to swallow. I finally did.

"This Tall Boy is good," I said and was lying. The Tall Boy came back up into my mouth and throat with every swallow. After two Tall Boys each, we drove over to the Crystal and got in the line of cars waiting to circle.

"Those are all redneck cars, Roddoh!" Duncan said and pounded on the steering wheel. With two Tall Boys in me, I was having more fun than I ever had in my life. We were in the line waiting to start circling the Crystal. Once we got in, it took twenty minutes to make one circle because everybody was slowing down to look at everybody else.

Duncan said: "Oh my God, Roddoh, look at all the pussy!" Socks was reading his Arabian Nights and tapping the dashboard with his fingers as if he was listening to music. The glow from underneath the Crystal's carport made it look like we were sitting inside Nana's refrigerator with the door open. The teenagers were leaning out their car windows looking at each other. Every few minutes a redneck gunned his engine, his tires squealed and the car jerked ahead just a little.

Duncan explained that whenever a Tennessee State Trooper pulled over a redneck out on the Loop, the redneck laughed and took off. Most of the time the Trooper didn't even bother to chase them because the redneck made their engine bigger than the Trooper's. The Trooper knew that.

Socks stopped reading and said, "That's exactly right. John Law won't give chase."

Duncan said the rednecks tested their new engines by letting the Troopers chase them and took Tennessee Avenue straight out from the street light in the middle of town up into the mountains with the Trooper's sirens wailing and their lights flashing trying to catch up.

"They don't care, Roddoh. They just want to test their engines."

Socks said, "And they'll drown their children if it isn't a boy."

"Listen to Socks, Roddoh," Duncan yelled and pounded the steering wheel. "Tall Boys, Roddoh! Tall Boys!" I pounded the back of the seat. I had two Tall Boys in me.

"Everybody who lives out on that Loop or up on the hills knows about baby drowning." Socks said.

Duncan pointed and said: "Oh my God, Roddoh. There's Barn Woman."

Socks said, "I'm getting out."

Barn Woman got in the car and said, "Woo Woooo Y'all!" Socks got out with his Quart and kept reading as he walked away. I was starting to feel dizzy.

We moved the Comet out of the line of circling cars and kept drinking Tall Boys. Duncan turned around and said, "Have I got a big surprise for you, Roddoh!" He drove over to the Methodist Church parking lot, the back door opened, and Ginger Rose jumped in. Duncan had planned it all along. I started laughing and vomited up a little Tall Boy into my mouth. Suddenly I was in the back seat with Ginger Rose and very glad it was her and not anybody else. I still didn't have hairs, but after finishing my second Tall Boy and working on my third, I didn't care. I was able to talk to Ginger Rose for the first time in my entire life.

"Tall Boy, Tall Boy, Tall Boy Hubba Jubba." I imitated Socks then whispered into Ginger Rose's ear: "I don't care if Old May is after me."

Ginger Rose said, "listen to you," and tried to move her ear away, but I talked louder in a big deep voice:

"I don't care if I lost my peashooter and I don't care if there's a trap door in the garden that's going to open up and drag me down to *HEH-YULL*, to *HEH-YULL*. Well *how yew*, I'm just fine, *how yew? Well, how yew?*"

I started practicing my *how yews how yews* right in Ginger Rose's ear but she pushed me away. That's when I saw Ginger Rose's titties and knew she had hairs. I called out: "Bob White Bob White oo oo oo oo oo."

Duncan said, "Ole Roddoh," and pounded the steering wheel.

I had to vomit.

Duncan said, "Roll down the window, Roddoh."

I was just able to roll it down and lean out as far as I could by the time we had pulled up at the stoplight on Main Street. I could see the road right below me and part of the curb. On the curb was four sets of shoes: Two little pairs and two big pairs, and legs. I couldn't wait and vomited in front of the four sets of shoes. We pulled away with the tires screeching and my head out the window, the strings of vomit flapping in the wind behind the car like cake batter dripping off a spoon. Ginger Rose pulled me back in and everything was spinning and I couldn't see or hear. I don't know what happened to Ginger Rose but remembered her laughing. I don't remember what we talked about but knew we had talked.

~

Later that week the cousins got into trouble with Old May. Shaw was leaving and wanted to do one last dangerous dare. We all sat up in the dogwood trees and shot peas down at her as she twisted up the driveway. I didn't want to do anything to Old May anymore. I just wanted to sit on my dogwood branch while she passed underneath, close my eyes and try to hear her transistor radio.

Old May looked like a walking hornet's nest. When we had thrown dogwood seeds down on Old May before, she'd swatted them away as if they were flies but had always kept walking. This time, she stopped, turned and looked up at us with her good eye. What she said was easy to understand:

"You little assholes. I'm telling my brother about what you did, and he's going to come and blow all of your shit away."

When Old May pulled out her knife, we jumped out of the dogwoods and ran as fast as we could. Old May took after us and even though she moved and twisted slowly, she kept coming. We ran over to where Munro was finishing our tree house, climbed up the ladder he had built and laid flat on the row of two by fours he'd nailed between two of Nana's Oaks. Munro talked to Old May while she stood right below us. She told Munro in a loud voice to let us know she was going to tell her brother about what we did and that her brother was going to come up to Nana's house the next morning and shoot us with his shotgun. Old May lowered her voice and spoke to Munro quietly. We couldn't hear anything she said. After that, she started shouting again.

"I'm telling my brother about what you-uns did, and he'll be coming up here and shotgunning all you little assholes. And sure enough, he'll stay up here until every last one of you is dead. I know y'all can hear every word I'm saying."

Old May turned and walked slowly back to the driveway and on up to the house to deliver her papers. Munro's face was red as the inside of a watermelon and said that Old May had shown him her knife and told him how she was going to gut us all after we were dead.

"That is no joke and you goddamn well shouldn't be teasing her. I'm going to have to tell your grandmother what her brother is planning on doing. The Vanover's don't care whose grandchild you are. I've known that woman my entire life, and she'll make good on what she says."

The cousins ran back into Nana's house and didn't say anything to Nana or anybody about Old May or her brother. Shaw and the Twins were leaving that afternoon, so we all had to get ready to say goodbye. Duncan had left the day before.

My mother told me, *You're saying a lot of goodbyes this week. It's going to be a real tugger.*

~

After Shaw, Hilda and Tilda left, my mother took Cameron and Lillian to Rexall to get sparklers for their last night in Tennessee. My mother knew what had happened with Old May and told me to go straight upstairs, stay in my room and not come out until she got back. She would pick me out a box of sparklers.

By the time I got back upstairs, Nana was lying in bed with

235

her reading glasses on, snoring, her mouth wide open. I crept around the banister as quietly as I could. At the end of the hallway, I noticed the lights of my mother's circular mirror had been switched on, and her bag of cotton was laying on the floor. I turned and walked across the hall. I had already taken one step into my room before I saw Clyne laying in the middle of the bed. He was curled up and playing with my green army men and had wrapped cellophane tape around his hand with my mother's cotton balls underneath. There was a trickle of blood down the side of his face coming out of the hole where his ear had been. Clyne had taken everything out: my Army, Navy, Air Force and Marine Corps pamphlets as well as all my baseball cards. The green Army men were lined up on the windowsill. When he saw me, Clyne knocked the army men off the sill using the back of his hand.

He was holding Mickey Mantle in his right hand and Boog Powell in his left, the one that was missing a finger. He dropped Boog Powell on the bed and I saw then the Bobby Orr was laying in front of him as well. I wasn't sure he had noticed Bobby Orr, since he was hockey.

I said, "That's Mickey Mantle."

"Uncle Murry worked over in Picher with Mutt Mantle, so we Presleys know who Mickey Mantle is, dumb shit." Clyne put Mickey Mantle in his shirt pocket. "You think you're better?"

I said, "No." I never heard of Mutt Mantle.

"I took care of that two-timing Kezia."

Clyne held his hand wrapped with my tape up in the air and said, "And I'll be taking daddy's truck over to

Knoxville and joining the goddamn Army."

My Uncle Andy had already said the Army wasn't going to take Clyne. I wondered if Clyne was going to bring Mickey Mantle with him when he went over there to try.

"I'll be getting myself double pussy at o-eight hundred from my cheating wife's sisters. After that, her family will be following her down to hell, I can tell you that. And now it's come time to take your eyes then I'll go down the hall and take your granny's eyes so I can wear them all around my neck when they're pinning on my sergeant stripes. You're the weak link that should have been drowned as soon as you were born. It's the powerful ones that lead the people into battle." Clyne took out a pocket knife and opened it. I couldn't speak, and couldn't turn my head. My legs felt like they'd both been nailed to the floor. I thought about how I could control my nightmares and that was the only thing I could try to do now. I began reciting the Lord's Prayer.

As soon as I did that, Clyne turned his head and took a step away from the window. Over Clyne's shoulder, I saw Munro standing in the driveway next to his truck, wiping his forehead with a handkerchief. Clyne watched his father then reached up with his hand, pushed the side of his cheek in and chewed on it. I did that too. Clyne folded up his knife and put it in his pocket.

"I don't have time for your see-no-evil now because I have to watch over my Daddy," Clyne said. He moved back a little bit more away from the window. We both watched Munro standing in the driveway. He seemed to be looking for somebody.

Clyne turned and walked past me as if I wasn't there and kept walking down the hall, stopping to peer at Nana snoring in her bed. The stairs creaked as he descended. I heard the kitchen screen door slam. I didn't think they would let Clyne wear our eyes around his neck anyway while they were making him a sergeant and wondered if he really thought they would.

I didn't tell anybody Clyne had been inside Nana's house and felt like I wanted to go to sleep even though it was five o clock in the afternoon. Clyne had left me alone but had taken my Mickey Mantle and my Army pamphlet. He hadn't known how valuable Bobby Orr was or he might have taken him as well.

Clyne must have cut around the back of Nana's house and out through the woods by the sandbox. After Munro left in his truck, I walked across the hallway into my mother's room and looked out her window down into the garden. Old May was sitting in the gazebo, and I could hear her talking and yelling at the same time. I turned the crank to hear what she was saying a little better. I had never seen her sitting in the gazebo.

"Job Willoughby would have wanted that," she said and looked straight up at me standing in my mother's window. She pointed and raised her voice.

"I see your little shit-ass uprr. My brother's coming in the morning with his shotgun and finishing all this."

I stepped back from the window and felt vomit shoot up the middle of my chest into my throat. Even with one good eye, Old May saw everything.

20
OLD MAY'S BROTHER, LIGHTNING, BUZZARDS, AND TUBE SWALLOWING

On the morning Old May's brother was coming to blow our shit away, I opened my eyes and smelled gingerbread cooking. I swung my legs over the side of the bed and caught sight of the white frost spread over the front yard like cake icing. Before going downstairs, I craned my neck to check the driveway and the Florist Shop Road for any sign of Clyne, in case he had decided to do my see-no-evil after all before heading up to the Willoughby house to get his *double pussy at o-eight hundred from his cheating wife's sisters.* Lillian, Cameron and I were the only cousins left in the house, but they were heading back to North Carolina after lunch.

Nana finally opened the oven door and lifted the tray out with her mitt. Each of us took a piece of paper towel, peeled one gingerbread man off the pan and ran out the front door, across the drive and into the front yard. I wasn't thinking about getting shot or stabbed or having a see-no-evil while we stood nibbling on the frosted grass. After finishing, Cameron, Lilian and I went down to the end of the driveway to wait for Old May and her brother. Cameron and I kept watch on the road behind the stone pillar while Lillian kept an eye on the woods in case Old May decided to come at us from behind with a broken bottle or butcher knife.

Old May always came over the hill on Tennessee Avenue

at nine o clock to deliver her papers. Nine o'clock came, and Old May hadn't yet come. Lillian and Cameron had to go back up to the house to pack, but I stayed at the end of the driveway. I wanted to see Old May's brother coming to blow our shit away more than anything in the world. The wait seemed as long and as suspenseful as the wait had been for the Apollo capsule's hatch to open after splashdown on the Moon Mission Special Report.

As I waited, the sun got hotter, and the woods swelled. When the middle of the road finally began to bake and waver, a man appeared at the top of the hill. He wasn't wearing a shirt and walked step by step with his shotgun broken open over his arm like Chuck Connors. Old May followed him twenty feet behind, her bag filled with Press and Tribune, looking like she hadn't delivered a single paper but had only come to follow her brother that morning. The man's chest was white, his arms red and his eyes black.

The State Trooper car parked in front of the drive the day before was gone. Old May's brother had made it all the way down from the mines, through the middle of town and up Tennessee Avenue, walking slowly in the middle of the road with his shotgun broken open, without anybody stopping him.

I didn't wait for them to get any closer but turned and ran as fast as I could up the driveway and into the house to tell Lillian and Cameron that Old May's brother had finally come to kill us all, walking down the middle of Tennessee Avenue with his shotgun cracked open like the Rifleman. Lillian and Cameron had to keep packing because Aunt Dixie was going to be there in an hour to pick them up.

I cracked open Nana's front door and looked straight down the driveway under the dogwoods as Old May's brother walked past, still in the middle of the road, and not even bothering to turn his head. Old May followed without turning hers either. They both looked like they had forgotten all about the cousins. I wanted to go down to the end of the driveway and shout at them.

~

The next morning, I opened my eyes and remembered everything: Clyne pouring lye into the boy's mouth, the two bodies in the tadpole pond and Old May's brother walking slowly down the middle of Tennessee Avenue. My peashooter was still missing and I hadn't told anyone about any of it. Nana said the man who had the skull fracture was ok but mad as a hornet. I didn't ask why. I didn't say anything. My mother was right: Hell was on this earth, and I had woken up right smack in the middle of it.

With Lillian and Cameron back in North Carolina, my mother and I were on our own again. Nana was going to swallow her tube at the end of the week and told me again how glad she was that I'd be sitting beside her at the kitchen table when the time came.

Munro was standing beside his truck holding a Winston when I came out the front door after Cream of Wheat. He wasn't bothering to hide the cigarette dangling on the end of his finger but just stood, letting it burn. He looked like he was examining his truck tire then began wiping the back of his neck with one hand over and over as if trying to rub something off. I nodded to Munro. He didn't nod back or say anything, so I stood with him and we both looked at his tire. After a minute. Munro dropped the Winston, ground his shoe down into the gravel and said:

"Well."

Munro looked like he didn't know what to do with himself.

That whole week, storms moved over the house, and lightning struck so close to the Willoughby's place at the top of the hill that I couldn't even begin counting down after the flash until I heard the thunder. The thunder clapped at the same time as the flash most of the time now. Nana and I stood at the top of the stairs and watched the sheets of rain outside the upstairs' window. After every lightning flash and thunder clap, Nana gripped the banister and puffed air into her cheeks.

"Lawsie, that was a close one."

Nana turned the window crank wide open so that we could hear every clap or rumble. The rain came down so hard, the trees on the other side of the driveway first became gray then disappeared altogether.

We never knew how close the lightning was going to come and held our breaths, the thunder getting louder and louder, sounding like it did when the cousins pushed the front panel of Nana's basement dryer in and out. After the last storm passed and the clouds lifted, one of the most exciting things that ever happened in my life happened: Buzzards began circling over Nana's garden!

Whenever Nana took me around the Loop in the Olds, we

could see buzzards circling in the distance.

Just look at the buzzards over yonder.

Whenever there were buzzards in the air, I couldn't take my eyes off them. I turned to look out the back window of the Olds, following them wherever we drove. The buzzards never left our sight because they soared so high. I saw them circling while we visited my grandfather's grave on the other side of the highway then saw the same ones while we were parked at the Crystal or heading around the Loop. John Bass was in the Boy Scouts and had explained:

Buzzards are called by the smell. They hone in on it.

Buzzard's don't flap their wings; buzzards soar, Nana said.

Dear God, they're so ugly, my mother said.

Something big must have died up yonder.

Nana always pointed with her knuckle in the direction of the thing that had died. I followed Nana's knuckle and wanted her to drive as close as she could to the exact spot so I could get out of the Olds and stand at the center of the buzzard's circle.

~

On the day the rain stopped, I was looking out the kitchen screen door and saw three cats run into the garden. When I went upstairs and looked out the window at the top of the staircase, I saw two more cut across, which was more cats than I had ever seen at Nana's house at one time. Old May turned up the driveway with her papers right after that, so I went into Nana's room to ask her about the cats. She lay on her bed snoring so I moved over to her bedroom window and pressed my head against the screen to get a good look at Old May limping toward the house. Right before she came twisting up the path I saw one more black cat crouching low under the Comet then shooting out into the front yard. Old May came *hup hup HUPPING* along the path and stopped right underneath Nana's window. She didn't look up but started talking. Old May couldn't have known I was listening and peeking down at her but stopped just as she had stopped underneath the dogwood tree in the driveway. I understood Old May's words as clearly as I had understood Socks' words when he spoke to me after Clyne's rasping.

"My brother's havin' to haul her up one big goddamn truck full of saw dust. Mrs. Matthews has camphor but not near enough, and I'm not telling her a goddamn thing."

Old May made a few *hubba hubbas* then spoke again: "My brother told me he knew where to get walnut and I told Ponnie that, but she had that damn shotgun out and said I don't care what you do, the motherfucking cats will eat the eyes. I already knew the cats would eat everything in her house if she let them. Ponnie turned around and shot one of those damn cats and told me 'She hain't dead,' and I said, 'fuck you, Ponnie! She's dead as coal.'"

Old May twisted up the path and cut around back to put a copy of the Press and Tribune inside the screen door. I looked over my shoulder at Nana who was beginning to wake up.

"Nana?"

She opened her eyes. "Yes, HONEY!"

"Do you know who Ponnie is?"

"Why yes. That's what they've always called Jemima Willoughby: Ponnie. I don't know how they got to calling her that."

Ponnie was Lurch! There were no cousins to tell what I heard Old May saying so I decided to ask Nana to finish her Woodchopper story. She had fallen asleep before the exciting part at the Troll's bridge, and I wanted to hear what happened to the poor old Woodchopper and had been wondering what the Troll was going to do. Nana started telling me the story from where we had left off but fell asleep as soon as she started. I shook Nana's shoulder, and she came out of her sleep putting on the Troll's deep voice:

"'I want your crosscut saw.'

The old Woodchopper used his crosscut saw to cut down the biggest trees in the forest. His crosscut saw, and his red ax were the only possessions that poor old Woodchopper had in the entire world. They were so precious to him that he kept them by his side at all times.

He told the Troll, 'I only have one saw, Troll and can't cut down trees without it. I need to sell my wood in town to buy food for my family to last us the winter.'

What the Woodchopper didn't tell the Troll was that the Woodchopper's family hardly had a thing to eat. The poor Woodchopper had been forced to sell the wood he had chopped so far which wasn't close enough to what he needed for the upcoming winter. He would buy as much food as he could in town and bring it all back on his wagon through the forest. The Woodchopper loved his children and wife more than anything else in the whole world and worked day and night cutting down trees with his crosscut saw then chopping them up with his favorite red ax. But the old Troll didn't care about the Woodchopper's family. He said, 'I want your crosscut saw.'"

Nana started snoring, but woke up just as quickly and said,

"Oh, Honey, it's come time I swallow that old tube again first thing tomorrow morning. It's so comforting to know you're going to be with me in the kitchen."

Nana started snoring again. I didn't wake her up but went down the hallway into my mother's room to try and catch a glimpse of Old May twisting along the Florist Shop Road after delivering the Tribune to Perseus. What I saw instead was Old May sitting on the gazebo bench for the second time in a row. I was very curious as to why she was doing that, moved downstairs and out the back door to stand just behind the back-porch post. I watched Old May until it began to get dark.

All night long I worried about nothing else but tube swallowing and didn't remember any dreams when I woke. When I got downstairs, my mother was already sitting on a folding chair in the kitchen doorway. My mother could never stand tube swallowing and always sat by the door, as far away from Nana as she could get. When Nana caught sight of me, she patted the chair next to hers. Storms had passed through in the night. Wind rattled the screen door.

After Nana set everything up, there was always the wait while she sat in her chair. On the red and white checked table cloth, she placed her green quart of ginger ale, her glass filled with ice, her large mixing bowl, her tub of Crisco, her towel and the box with her tube inside. Nana finally opened the box, said, "well," then stood up. That was the signal. This time, Nana looked down at her tube and said,

"Mercy. Sometimes the pain gets so strong I don't know if I can pull that ole tube out after it hits bottom."

"Mother," my mother said, her voice going up. "Mmm mm."

Nana said: "Thank you for coming, Rodney, I couldn't do this without you. I'm going to fix you a nice big bowl of Cream of Wheat as soon as we get through."

"Oh mother, I can fix his Cream of Wheat."

Nana poured ginger ale into the glass with ice, lifted the tube out of its box, rubbed Crisco along the bottom half then gripped the other end with her towel. She stepped away from the kitchen table and stood with both her legs planted in the middle of the kitchen floor, lifted the tube up into the air and let it drop all the way down her throat. She coughed with the tube inside, lifted it up and out, took two steps back over to the table, dropped the tube in its box and lowered herself down into her chair. She started drinking ginger ale and spitting up blood into the mixing bowl. I felt a whole lot better with Nana spitting up blood and drinking ginger ale. Tube swallowing was over.

"Look here, Rindy, I'm going to fix Rodney two nice pieces of cinnamon toast and a nice big bowl of Cream of

Wheat."

Nana got up and moved over to the oven.

"Mother, sit! You just swallowed your tube."

In a few minutes, Nana handed me two pieces of cinnamon toast hot out of the oven. I had also just finished a nice big bowl filled with Cream of Wheat. I took my cinnamon toast, ran outside and jumped off the front porch. I was so glad that tube swallowing was over. With Clyne nowhere to be seen, I felt like I could fly and wasn't afraid of anything.

21
THE BIGGEST DARE OF THEM ALL
AND SOME GOOD HOT ROLLS

A buzzard shot over the top of Nana's roof, gliding across the driveway, not flapping but swooping and swiveling then disappearing into a cloud that had been pulled down over the pines like a hat. The dogwoods looked like they wanted to run away but couldn't. The wind had them pinned halfway to the ground.

I listened to the gravel under my feet as I ran along the Florist Shop Road, turned and cut straight down into the garden, still holding my cinnamon toast. I stopped halfway down the steps and gobbled both pieces while examining Snow White in the cat grass, the rust on her wires making it look as if she were bleeding. I walked the rest of the way down the steps, straight past the gazebo and up into the woods. This was the first time in my life I had gone on the other side of the gazebo. I stopped and listened:

Wuh chew wuh chew.

Dad would have said *interesting*, and might have even added, *odd*. There was only one bird chirping in the entire forest.

The very next step, I slipped on a patch of wet leaves and landed on both hands. After that, I kept turning my head, examining the ground for wet leaves, snakes, or dook, picking my feet up like a Tennessee Walker as I began to climb the hill. The farther I moved up, the more buzzards

249

I glimpsed soaring over the tops of the trees with even more circling like black paint smudges in the blue sky between the gray clouds.

Perseus told Nana that the hog at the top of the hill had most likely died and that his rotten body had called the buzzards. The hog they had buried in the pit at the church picnic last summer had been as big as a full-grown man, so I wasn't surprised that this one called in so many buzzards.

I smelled the dead hog as soon as I started up the hill; at first, only when the breeze brought it past my nose; higher up, it brushed my face as if someone had draped wet clothes soaked in the smell over the tree branches. Even further still, the smell worked its way into my mouth, as if poured in and was worse than sour milk. Vomit shot up through the back of my throat more than once and I had to hold one nostril at a time to blow the pieces out before starting again. The smell was always in front of me after that, as if I had been sitting at the kitchen table and someone had sprinkled sugar over a pan of diarrhea, baked it in the oven, then dished it out onto a plate.

The woods never seemed to end. The birds stayed quiet. W*u chew wu chew* was the only living song I heard until half way up when a bobwhite called. I stopped and held my breath. There was no answer. In standing still, the smell grew stronger, as if the smell had stepped out from behind a tree and was raising an ax above its head. I had to move.

When one of the grey clouds was pushed away by the wind, a bucket of white and orange light was dumped over the woods in front of me. I saw the buzzard swoop in over the pine right above, an old wrinkled gray man with a little black eye. The top of the hill ahead looked like the deck of an aircraft carrier now with the buzzards flying in low, landing then taking off. I became more excited than I had ever been in my life. I was getting closer and closer to the center of the buzzards' circle.

In front of me about ten feet, through the gap where the trees ended, stood a little shack with a wooden fence around it. Dirt and dust sprayed out from between two slats and shook a stalk of ragweed. In the gap over those same slats, his two eyes looked as black as the end of a shotgun barrel. The hog wasn't dead. He snorted twice more, blowing the ragweed all the way over to the ground. The hog had been standing stock still, watching me the whole time, his eyes pressed against the gap between the wood like a German Soldier looking out of his pillbox through binoculars, waiting until I got close enough to open fire. I took a few steps more and could now see his nostrils opening and closing.

A line of buzzards sat along the roof of the lopsided house behind the hog pen. The house looked like one of Nana's quilts, put together with different sized strips and colors of plywood or aluminum or plastic. I crouched against one of the last trees before the clearing, listening to the hog breathe. He smelled like wet leather, better than what was hanging in the air. No other cousin had seen the hog and no other cousin could understand what it was like to stare him full in the face or could have even begun to guess what it was like to be wrapped up in the smell at the top of the hill.

Perseus had told the cousins: *If you see the hog pen, turn the hell around. That hog doesn't give a goddamn about you or anybody else.*

I didn't turn around. I wanted to touch the Willoughby's

house and stand underneath the center of the buzzard's circle. The hog kept staring at me without snorting and looked like he knew why I was there and that he may have even been expecting me. The hog was as big as Munro's truck. I didn't think he could get out of his pen but wasn't sure. The way he looked at me through the wooden slats was as if to say he knew a lot more about hogs and hog pens than I did.

To relax the hog, I pretended that I was looking at something. I picked up a leaf and turned it over, the whole time pretending I was examining the leaf very carefully. The hog snorted, looked down at his hooves as if expecting there might be a leaf waiting there for him as well but looked up almost as soon as he looked down, pushed his snout through the slats, and snorted twice as loud as he had before. I had tricked the hog, and he understood that I had tricked him and was letting me know.

We stared at each other, and during the split second when our eyes met, I heard everything in the woods from near and far. The birds were all speaking when they hadn't spoken before.

Dee dee Dee dee

Dwee dohh Dwee dohh

Bob White. Bob White. Bob Bob Bob Bob.

The woods became so loud that I had to turn my eyes away from the hog and look up, trying to find space. The birds chattered and the thick green leaves around me quivered. The trees were listening and waiting for something to happen. The birds were telling both them and me what that something was. The trees might have understood. I didn't but again heard the hog breathing as well as a tiny noise behind his pen: A plate scrape once. I moved sideways along the last row of trees. As I moved, the hog moved as well, following me like a State Trooper, marching along the inside of his pen, glaring as if he wanted to write me a speeding ticket. I examined the hog pen fence to make sure there wasn't an open door. I didn't trust the hog and could tell he didn't like it I was there.

Things were laying on the mud at the bottom of his pen, like toys. I couldn't see what those things were. A belt sat on top of a slop pile, not mixed in with it but dropped there, along with some clothes. I didn't have time to examine those things while the hog was following me and snorting.

I stepped out from behind the hog pen fence and as soon as I saw the house, a buzzard took off from the edge of the woods, skimming the top my hair and flapping its wings. I ducked and heard a plate scrape again.

Between the edge of the woods and house lay a dead dog and two dead cats. The cats lay on their backs, legs sticking straight up, dirt and fur packed together, both looking to be growing out of the ground. The dog lay on its side and had been tied to a post with an old rope collar still around its neck. The dog's tongue hung out of its mouth with ants were using it as a road. More buzzards circled than I had ever seen in my life. Buzzards sat in the trees, lined up on the hog pen fence and all the way across the little house's roof. They weren't paying attention to anything in particular. One of them fluttered a wing. That was it. They stayed still, waiting. The hog had his back turned, pushing his head into the mud, snorting then pushing his head in again.

The smell was so close, as if it stood beside me, whispering. I turned but saw nothing. I hopped over the dog to the side of the house and stood beside a small window, gray as Munro's truck windshield from his Winstons. I pressed my back flat against the wall not wanting the Willoughby sisters to catch me on their property. The smell burned my eyes and skin as if I was standing in front of a roaring fire. I waved my hand in front of my face then held my breath and waited for a breeze. The smell flew right in front of me like a black scarecrow and I flinched.

The dare was over and I wasn't sure if I was ever going to tell Shaw that I'd done it. He would only believe what I said if he had been with me the whole way up, followed by the smell as I had been followed. He would have had to vomit up into his mouth as I had vomited up and stand up against the house with his eyes burning, seen the dead dog, the two dead cats and ducked when buzzards sliced through the air over his head like bullwhips cracking.

I heard another scrape inside the house then *clink clink*. I stayed still, waiting, and looked down to check if there was dog doo on my shoes. There wasn't. The smell was confusing, sweet and rotten, and my stomach jerked up into my chest, so high I couldn't bring it back down.

A new shotgun shell lay between the dead dog and the house. I wanted to put it in my pocket but wasn't sure what might have crawled into its open end. My clothes felt like they were moving and the smell had worked its way underneath.

Stacks of Press had been piled against the side of the house, wrapping around the corner out of sight, with more newspapers in the woods, white mushrooms growing on top of those.

An empty can of cream corn and an empty can of Lima beans lay right beside the two dead cats then more cream corn cans farther away by the edge of the woods, most of them half buried. The buzzards circled low now and landed all around me, more of them waiting on the ground than had been there when I had first showed up. The sky was clear blue. The breeze had gone. I pressed my back against the wall of the house and examined all of it, trying to locate the center.

The smell hummed, my head began to swell and I had to sit down. Another breeze made the hum louder still, and I vomited into my mouth another time and stood up quick, so it wouldn't fall onto my pants. I felt better after I let it go and rolled my head over, placing my eye over the window pane. Kezia was sitting on an old brown couch in the center of the room. Her teeth stuck straight out, and her titties pushed through her shirt but weren't as big as they had been when I saw them by the sandbox. I shut my eyes tight then opened them. The smell against the window burned and I saw the bottom pane had been cracked.

The smell was coming through the crack in the window, from inside the Willoughby sister's house.

I was able to open one eye and see the two teeth left in Kezia Willoughby's top row. Her bottom row was bared all the way to her wisdom teeth, her lips pulled up and back as if hooks were attached. She tilted over to one side, leaning on a stack of Press and looked as if she was going to fall off the couch any second.

Against the far wall stood a wooden statue of a thin man wearing a work shirt buttoned all the up to the collar, brown work pants and black shoes with their laces tied. The statue's arms were hung straight down tight against his side. He stood at attention and staring straight at me from across the room. Even though his face had been painted brown and shined, I knew the man as soon as I saw him. At his feet was the can of polyurethane Nana kept on the floor of her pantry. This statue of a man had been polyurethaned. He shined as bright as Nana's den floor or my room's window sill. Another brand new can of polyurethane sat at Kezia's feet with a paintbrush resting on the lid.

Before I could duck, the younger sister Stib walked up to Kezia and stood in front of her holding a bowl in one hand and a spoon in the other.

"She wants more cream corn."

I jumped when Lurch's voice boomed just behind the wall. I couldn't see Lurch, but her voice rattled an aluminum panel beside my head. Stib put the spoon in the bowl, scooped up cream corn and held it in front of her sister. Stib looked around and didn't seem to be paying attention to where the spoon was.

"Give it to her!"

I jumped. Lurch's voice was louder still. The glass beside my head hummed. Cream corn was sliding down Kezia's face, spilling off her chin and onto her dress as well as dripping off her arm onto the stack of Press. Her shoes sat in a puddle of creamed corn. Stib stuck the spoon all the way into Kezia's mouth. Kezia didn't chew and Stib pulled the spoon out, cream corn coming out with it. I heard *crack* and jerked my head around but saw nothing but buzzards creeping between the trees. I wanted to go now but couldn't run out in the open with Lurch somewhere behind the window. I pressed my back flat against the outside wall, turned my head over one more time, and saw Kezia's hair rise into the air then fall straight back down onto the top of her head. As soon as Kezia's hair dropped, there came tapping against the window pane: Flies. After the first few taps, I jerked my head away because a wave of flies smacked the glass, like a bucket of them had been tossed and I heard the buzzing like a bee hive. One or two flies squeezed through the crack and I batted them away. Flies were everywhere and I had to squat again, the smell so strong, it itself buzzed. I couldn't tell the difference between sound and smell and it had all gotten worse and I was hearing everything, this time twice as loud; all the birds, and all the leaves moving in the woods; the buzzards fluttering their wings along the fence that I hadn't heard before; behind it all the summer hum, as loud as it had ever been, as if where I stood was the place it came from. In and around the weeds and high grass and golden rod, where the sun cut across the side of the hog pen, everything was shaking, not just quivering. I rose, turned and had one more look inside the house.

Kezia's hair was all flies!

I fell over backward when a yellow light flashed on the other side of the glass, almost landing on the dog. Lurch's big head moved in front of the pane so quickly I couldn't duck out of sight. She stared at me, her yellow bow as big as a Christmas wreath flopping down over her face. I got up to run as a buzzard dropped off the roof and cut over the dog, causing me to trip. One foot slid out from under me so I had to put one hand down right in the middle of the dog as if the dog was made of pudding. With my hand stuck inside, I turned back to see yellow paint smear along the inside of the Willoughby's little greasy gray window. The yellow bow followed Lurch, both disappearing as if a light had been turned off. I pushed myself up out of the dog hearing pots fall onto the floor inside and Lurch yelling Praise God this and Praise God that. As soon as I started to run again, my foot jammed straight into the dog's chest, and I found it hard to yank it out and when I did, slipped, this time because the dog's intestines wrapped around my ankle as if the dog wanted to hold on.

The hog was shaking something back and forth in its mouth when I got over to the pen. I slowed to wipe my foot against the fence post watching the big frog's head the hog had clenched between its teeth. The hog had eaten the inside of the big bullfrog and all that was left was the skin dangling below his chin. The hog stopped what it was doing and snorted. In his pen were a pair of torn pants and another shotgun casing. When the hog turned its head a little more, I could see that the bull frog's head he was holding had hair. The hog kicked an empty can of cream corn with his hoof and snorted again. The can of cream corn rolled right on top of my Mickey Mantle. I stopped altogether:

The hog had my Mickey Mantle.

I got a better look at the face the hog was holding. He turned toward me and shook it first back and forth then up and down as if to say: *Look at what I am playing with.*

When the hog started to jerk the face up into its mouth, bite by bite, I heard *POW* and slipped again, this time right onto my hands and saw the ground beside the hog pen was covered in creamed corn that I hadn't seen before because I'd been keeping an eye on the hog.

Lurch stood at the edge of the woods, her yellow bow flopping from side to side, firing her shotgun into the air. She squinted, like Mister Magoo but didn't see me at the other end of the hog pen fence.

I was used to being chased in my nightmares, so I hopped sideways and ran around and through the trees, heading straight down the hill, falling on my hands, getting up, the branches, leaves, and sticks smacking me in the face over and over. I rested only once the whole way down, hiding behind an Oak, holding my breath. I didn't hear anything coming after me but didn't wait to start running again. The farther down the hill I ran, the happier and happier and happier I became because I knew I had finished the biggest dare of them all.

By the time I got all the way down to the garden, the woods again were dark green with blackness between the leaves and Old May sitting in the gazebo, examining her own hands. She twisted around, stared at me with her good eye for a moment, turned back and continued examining her hands. She turned them over and over. I heard music so soft that crickets could be playing it.

A stack of the Press sat beside her on the gazebo bench. On top of the newspapers, side by side, was a yellow transistor radio and my peashooter. I stood still as a statue and listened:

"These boots are made for walking, and that's just what they do. . . One of these days these boots are gonna walk all over you. . ."

Old May picked up a can of peas off the bench and took a spoon up in the other. She began chewing and humming at the same time. When the song ended, Old May cocked her head, looked straight at me with her good eye, and said,

"You hear the bees humming beside the honeysuckle. They touch down and touch down and touch down then touch down."

~

"Lawsie Mercy," Nana said. "They found plates of food on the couch and over twenty years of Press piled up around the house as if they had been stacking wood."

I had seen Stib feeding cream corn to her dead sister and watched Kezia's hair take off and land. No one in the world had seen what I had seen or knew that I had seen it except the hog and Lurch although Old May looked like she might have known. I hadn't told a soul about what I had seen and wasn't going to. I wasn't going to write down what I saw on Dad's yellow pad, at least not now; I'd have to wait and for the time being, only write down what I heard other people say.

My mother talked to Adair on the hall phone the whole next day and even though Adair was calling from Nashville, she knew more about what happened up there at the top of the hill than my mother did because Uncle Andy was friends with the same Sheriff's Deputy who had smelled Kezia out of the window of his patrol car. Mr. Bass had called them when he heard a shotgun go off. Only I knew that had been Lurch firing into the air at the edge of the woods after seeing me peeking through their kitchen window.

The Deputy had driven up Tennessee Avenue with his window open and smelled it then stuck his head out and saw the buzzards.

Aunt Adair's voice had been so loud that my mother held the phone away from her ear so I could hear everything she was saying.

"They found Kezia sitting right on the living room couch, and they think she had been dead for a week and thought Munro's son had killed her, but we don't know that. Andy thinks he found out what she was up to and took it out on her. Jemima forced Stib to treat Kezia as if she were still alive. Now they have a state-wide manhunt out for Clyne but Clyne's gone. They can't find him. You still need to be very careful."

I wasn't worried. The hog had eaten Clyne and saved his face for desert. Only I knew that. No one else in the world did. If the State Troopers looked in the hog pen, they might find Mickey Mantle, but wouldn't find Clyne. The hog wasn't going to tell them where Clyne was.

Old May was done for the summer and wasn't coming after me. I'd heard and seen her yellow transistor playing. I wanted her to keep my peashooter.

I knew the creamed corn Stib had been feeding her sister

was from Nana's pantry. Nana had been given the Willoughby sisters her extra cream corn for years and years. Nana always called it *good ole creamed corn*.

"They were just feeding her mother's cream corn," Aunt Adair said.

"NO, Adair, they weren't feeding her mother's cream corn, were they? As if she was still ALIVE? Mother's cream corn?"

My mother's voice rose to almost a squeak. She already knew it had been Nana's creamed corn they were feeding her and already knew they had pretended Kezia was alive. She heard the same story from Jo Ann Bass about an hour before Adair called but let Adair go through the whole thing again. Adair knew that the statue standing against the wall in the Willoughby sister's living room was the polyurethaned body of Job Willoughby, their daddy. When their daddy died, the Willoughby sisters pretended he was alive too and may still have been pretending.

"They polyurethaned his body from head to toe, Rindy, and dressed him in his favorite pair of overhauls. They think they had him propped up in the living room for ten years. The Sheriff's deputy told Andy that they believed the sisters were fixing to polyurethane Kezia."

"Dear GOD, Adair! And with mother's polyurethane from the pantry!?"

After the telephone calls, I had gone out to the sandbox and spent the rest of the day melting Army men onto my German Messerschmitt. By the time my mother called me in for dinner, two Sheriff's cars had parked on the Florist Shop Road with their lights turning. When I came through the front door, my mother whispered to me that Old May had told Nana about something she'd seen in the garden. Nana called the Sheriff after she heard what it was.

"I don't want even to think about what's down there in Tinker Bell's Fountain," my mother said.

Nana, my mother and I sat in the little room overlooking the Florist Shop Road and the garden. After tube swallowing or her knee injections, Nana liked to have a special dinner in that room. She had fixed us meatloaf that night with gravy and mashed potatoes. With the sun setting, the red lights at the top of the patrol cars flashed across the garden and the white nubs of fallen dwarves turned red. I had to squint to see what the Deputies were doing because the rays of the setting sun cut across the screen like someone had thrown a carton of milk against it. I saw one deputy wearing chest-high wading boots standing up in the middle of the tadpole pond holding a pole.

"Rodney, you look like you're ready for another roll."

From her seat by the window, Nana shook the roll basket at me. I was craning my head to try and see the garden over her shoulder when Nana turned and pulled the curtain closed.

"We'll just let them finish what they need to do and eat ourselves some of this good dinner," Nana said. "Hand me your plate and let me dish you some more good cream corn. Rindy Anne, pass Rodney's plate to me."

My mother handed Nana my plate. She ladled cream corn on and *clacked* her spoon. My mother took the plate back and set it down in front of me. Nana moved the roll basket to one side so she could see better. Then she slid the centerpiece over so she could get an even better view of my plate.

"Just pass your glass down here and let me pour you some more of this good iced tea."

Nana filled my glass before I could tell her *I'm ok*. She made the tea in a pitcher the night before and used clove, lemon, and Domino sugar then put it in the refrigerator overnight.

"Oh Honey, let me have your plate one more time," Nana said. "Because it sure looks like you'll be needing another one of these good rolls."

Nana held the roll basket and shook it at me.

"And I'll cut you another slice of meat loaf right quick."

"Nana, I'm OK."

"Well then let me at least put another spoonful of these good Lima beans right down on that plate of yours."

The wooden spoon *clack-clacked* and Nana moved the centerpiece all the way over to the end of the table with the back of her hand. She pushed a big spoonful of cream corn into her mouth and watched me eat.

ABOUT THE AUTHOR

A.F Knott has worked as a surveyor in the offshore oil industry, a lunch deliverer, a paper broker, a cyclotron engineer and a doctor. Ramonst is his second novel. He has two sons and lives in England. Visit him and his blogs at www.afknott.com